Power of Honesty
Poweress Series Book 3

By Minniel Douglas

Dedication:

To my Husband, who has walked this journey of love and marriage with me, who has shown me support and love along the way. Thank you for taking this journey to create a marriage that would be pleasing to God and a blessing to us and our children.

To my Children, who have shown me unconditional love, in a way that only those who are born from your womb can. Thank you for allowing me to be your Mommie and allowing me to love you. Thank you for showing me that this creativity that lives within me lives in you both. You guys are my gifts, and I am so blessed to have you.

To our marriage Counselor, you know who you are. We would not be where we are had you not allowed us to experience your gift and skill of marriage counseling. Our marriage is a better because you helped us become a 'We' and not 'a He or an I.' Thank you for your love and continual support.

To my Mommie, who is always in my corner cheering me on. You help me every day in ways I cannot even explain with words. Thank you for your love and for showing me how to love.

Last, but not least, thank you to all the Readers of the Poweress Series so far. All of the love, support, and reviews you send are genuinely awe-inspiring. Your enthusiasm and eagerness for the next book drive me to continue to seek God for more words to write and stories to tell. You guys encourage me more than you know. Thank you for reading, and please continue to share.

Copyright

Note:

This title is a standalone; however, please take a moment and read the other titles in the series.
This title is also for adults only. It contains some themes, actions, and language that may be offensive to some.

Table of Contents

Poweress:

The act of walking in the Divine Feminine Power that God has given you to become exactly who He has created you to be.

Chapter 1: Liza

One year ago

"When was the first time you met Dante?" My therapist, Dr. Judy, asked me.

The truth is, there is no way I could forget. I remember the moment vividly because that moment changed my life in the most delicious way. I was a freshman at the Xavier University of Louisiana and a chemistry major. My entire life, I had been the "sexy nerd." You know, the one who was all into her books but was gorgeous and knew how to enjoy a party to some extent. Anyway, I went to Xavier because I needed to get away from home, which was in Houston, TX. I wanted to change my image and loosen up a bit. My best friend Lyric always told me I should "really act like myself." With Lyric, I am always outspoken and fun. I think with others, I tend to go into my shell. Anyway, I went to college intending to change that. The first night at Xavier, I remember thinking I should have gone to Clark Atlanta with

Lyric, but no, I wanted to be different. So, I was in New Orleans, alone.

Back to meeting Dante. I decided to go to a party with my suitemate. It was at one of the exclusive clubs in the French Quarter. Everyone is always excited about what is happening on Bourbon Street. When really, the action is about what is happening above it. Most of the old buildings that people assume are restaurants and apartments are not. They are exclusive clubs for the New Orleans Elite. I, like everyone else, had no idea about this until I started talking to my suitemate. She was an upperclassman and native of New Orleans. Her parents had been members of one of the Clubs for generations. She talked me into coming with her to one of the events and its after-party.

That night, I arrived at the dead-end of an alley off Bourbon Street that housed a black door in the corner. This was the exact address that my suitemate gave me. The black door had a purple cross over the doorknob. I knocked in the 3-set patterned as she had told me, and when the door opened, I gave the code word *Peaches* to the bouncer. He eyed me slowly as I walked past him, but he said nothing. Inside there was a black hall lined with mirrors on the ceiling. At the end of the hall was a red door with a purple cross over the doorknob. I knocked in the 4-set pattern that my suitemate gave me, and when the door opened, the most beautiful woman I had ever seen stood in the doorway. She was wearing a gold satin mermaid dress with her hair pulled high into a bun and accented with a diamond broch. Her blackwood skin shimmered like an otherworld goddess. Then she said in a sultry voice, "Welcome to Chateau LeBlanc."

She closed the door behind her and stood in the hall staring at me. She waited like I was supposed to respond, but my suitemate, Christy, had not given me any more instructions. The beautiful lady arched a nicely manicured eyebrow, but I was stuck. I literally didn't know what to do. So, I said, "Hello."

She smiled at me and then turned to open and go back through the door, which I assumed meant she was kicking me out. Then Christy came up behind me wearing a cream-colored shirt with a fitted pencil skirt. Christy was pretty. She wore her hair in waves that cascaded down her back and had a luxurious color of red on her lips that matched her satiny brown skin perfectly. She smiled at me and then placed her hand on the arm of the beautiful lady and said, "Mother, this is my suitemate, Liza." The lady stopped and returned her attention back to me. She smiled gently and stated to Christy, "Darling, you forgot to give her the final instructions. To bring people into the Order, they need to know how to follow."

"My apologies. Can she try again?" Christy stated.

"Of course, Darling." With that, the beautiful lady turned and started walking through the red door. Then over her shoulder, she said "You have 5 minutes, Christelyn"

"Yes, Ma'am." After the lady turned down an invisible hall. Christy turned to me.

"Christy, what is she talking about joining the Order? I thought I came here for a party."

"Well, kind of. Look to get into the event you have to be a member or a prospective member. You are great and you have the intelligence, wit, and charm to make it in the Order. Trust me. I know it is a lot. But you will need these people to make it out here in New Orleans and a lot of other cities, like Houston. Our network runs deep. I promise there is nothing evil or crazy. There is no sexual exploitation or anything like that. Trust me?"

I took a breath. Part of me was like *no I don't trust you.* The other part was like *Liza what do you have to lose. This seems like one of those moments people either take the road that leads to destiny, or they choose mediocrity. I ain't come for mediocrity.* Then I heard that soft still voice of God say, "Trust me. Say OK." So, I said, "OK."

After I agreed she said, "Our club/order only takes members every 10 years. This year is an induction year. This is the party that determines if the rest of the members agree with your nomination for membership. Do you understand? Any questions?"

"Yes, I get it. Yes, lots of questions, but we don't have much time. Let's do this and I will ask later."

She laughed and then proceed to give me the rest of the instructions that she forgot to tell me earlier. After she was satisfied that I knew and understood her instructions, she walked me back down the black hall. She said I had to do it all over again as if I had just walked through the door with the guard.

"Liza, I promise you will not regret this."

I watched her make her way to the red door and once it was closed, I whispered. "God, I hope not. God help me."

I waited 5 minutes as instructed and then walked down the hall and made the 4-pattern knock again on the red door. This time the beautiful woman opened the door, ushered me in, and closed the door behind me. She didn't smile. She just said, "Welcome to Chateau LeBlanc."

"The pleasure of God follows they who dare listen," I stated in a low voice and then did a slight bow, just as instructed.

The beautiful woman smirked. "How will you proceed?"

"Through the narrow gate."

"Though it may be difficult?"

"Difficult is based on a premise without God. My journey is divinely ordered."

With that, she smiled brightly at me. I blew out a breath of relief.

"Liza, I am Lady LeBlanc, your journey begins tonight. Enjoy the festivities, for tomorrow the challenges begin." With that, she turned and had me follow her. We went through a series of hallways that seem to lead higher and higher, each hall was the same black walls with mirrored ceilings. We finally got to a hall where I could hear music playing. The closer we got to the end of the hall, the most radiant voice I have ever heard got clearer and clearer. It was a man, and his voice was deep like Barry but smooth like Luther but modern like *Him*. It was dripping with intensity, intellect, spice, and sex. I was falling for the voice alone. *Liza, get it together,* I said to myself.

At the end of the hall was a deep purple door, whereas all the other doors have been black or red. Lady LeBlanc put her hand on the doorknob, but before she opened it, she turned to look at me. The light from the soft spotlight above illuminated her eyes which were the color of milk chocolate. She asked, "I know my daughter equipped you quickly, so I will ask you, do you have any questions?"

"Actually one. Is there anything I should not say or do at this party?"

"No. Be yourself. Let your personality show. These are businessmen and women, leaders, and your peers. They are human just like you. We want authentic people and people who are willing to be themselves." She smirked again. "Any more questions?"

"Not right now."

"Ok then. Christelyn will be your guide through this process. Use her knowledge to your advantage. Don't be afraid to ask. It is better to know than not." She gave me a nod.

I nodded in return.

With that, she opened the purple door and light flooded the dark hallway. Crossing the threshold brought us into the most beautiful ballroom I have ever seen. As we walked, there were chandeliers and glass tables. Dark wood floors and exposed brick walls which held some of the most beautiful artwork. Each section of the room was like its own gallery having a detailed theme full of artwork, statues, and crystal decorative pieces. The room was deep, and glass bars were on all sides of the room. There was a bar in front of me, behind me, and on either side of me. There were ice sculptures of lions both male and female. It was immaculate. The people were all African American, like me and they were dressed gorgeously. I felt underdressed in my black dress with the little flare at the thigh and my faux Valentino's.

I let out a long breath. I really had no idea what I had gotten myself into. As I followed Lady LeBlanc, all eyes were on her. She was like a celebrity. Eventually, we made it to a cove with a velvet purple coach and a glass coffee table with a crystal paw as the base. The cove looked to be VIP. Christy was there and she smiled up at me. Then, the music started, and that voice started serenading me again. I closed my eyes and began to sway to the melody. I felt someone touch me. It was Christy.

"Hey, this is my Dad, but here he is Monsieur LeBlanc."

"Hello, Monsieur," I said with a small bow of the head as Christy had shown me. Her father was sexy as hell like if I liked old men and he wasn't married, he could have me now. I chuckled to myself. He nodded back to me and then said in the most mesmerizing voice "Hello Dear, truly a pleasure."

With that, Lady LeBlanc sat next to him, and they began to talk. Christy introduced me to other people in the VIP, but I kept getting distracted by the voice that was singing. I finished the conversation with one of the VIP members and asked Christy where the restroom was. As I made my way speaking nicely to all who I passed, the singer started singing "This Woman's Work" by Maxwell. That was it. I had to look. Until this point, I had been engaged with person after person in conversation. To be honest, I had not taken a view of the singer yet as I was trying not to swoon over whoever he was while I was supposed to be making a good impression. But when the singer hit that high note at the beginning of the song, I knew I was in for it. I had to look. So

I glided to a nearby wall, and I turned around slowly so as not to be noticeable. When I turned around to say I melted would have been a sheer understatement. I leaned into the wall a little more and took the singer in from head to toe, and Oh, My Gaud!!!!

Chapter 2: Liza

This man was all things delicious and dangerous. He was erotic, sensual, intelligent, and professional all at once. He was the color of pure ebony, like the darkness of night, with piercing eyes to match. I was too far to see their color, but he was staring dead at me, and the look of longing that passed his features ultimately had me stuck. I broke the stare we were entangled in and let my eyes travel down the slender point of his nose to the full brown lips on his face. His mouth was engulfed in the most lusciously moisturized black beard. It looked like it was soft to the touch. I wanted to run my fingers through its tresses. He licked his lips as he continued to croon the lyrics, singing in a voice that poured from behind the most beautiful set of teeth, "I know you have a little life in you, yet I know you have a lot of strength left...."

I continued to peruse his body with my eyes, taking in his broad shoulders and strong stance in his midnight blue tailored suit. He had on oxfords that matched his black shirt perfectly. His shirt was unbuttoned at the top enough to see the faint giving of his chest.

I was jolted from my thoughts as Christy came up to me and blocked my line of sight, and then moved to stand next to me.

"Gurl, I know. He gets all my friends."

I looked at her. She smiled. "That's my brother. My friends always swoon over him." She turned to me, so I did the same, not knowing what to say to her admission. "Look, Liza, I like you. So, I will say this. My brother is complicated. He doesn't do relationships much, and he usually sees my friends as off-limits." I arch an eyebrow in response. "However, the way he was looking at you just now, I am not so sure that that applies to you. The best advice I have is to let him come to you." With that, she patted my shoulder and then walked away to mingle with more guests.

It's crazy. This family of hers is all gorgeous. I did hear her loud and clear, though. The truth was, I was not sure if I wanted anything from this brother of hers anyway. I was just checking him out, after all. At least, I thought that was true. I went to the restroom and then came out and mingled.

Christy was not lying. The more people I met, the more I realized the kind of people surrounding me. We were talking about politicians, doctors, lawyers, pastors, professors, scientists, actors, literally any and everyone from all fields. It seemed like they kept coming to me in droves, and I would see Christy out the corner of my eye encouraging me to keep talking. Then I remembered Lady LeBlanc said to enjoy myself because the challenges started tomorrow if I was chosen. That thought brought all of this back into perspective. The people were coming to me in droves because they wanted to see if I was a good fit for their order. Christy had informed me, during one of the moments no one was surrounding me, that the vote for which candidates would be chosen would happen after the party tonight. Some electronic kind of voting system. The truth was, I was not sure who the other candidates were. I really couldn't tell. I went to the bar and ordered a glass of wine, prosecco of some brand. I was not really into brands. Honestly, I could get any brand I wanted since my parents were pharmaceutical chemists who owned a pharmaceutical company that made everything from erectile dysfunction meds to blood pressure meds to drugs that increased your energy and metabolism without thyroid activation. My parents were the best in the business. I just didn't feel the need to always flaunt a designer or pay attention to labels and brands. My parents said it would change when I got older, and being at this party helped me see why. There was every name brand you could think of in here. From the clothes the people wore to the bar to the décor, the place dripped in black wealth, and the fact that I was impressed with its opulence surprised me enough to have a drink.

As I stood there, I realized this bartender was giving me a drink without carding me. I did have a fake ID since my 19-year-old self could not get a drink regularly. As this thought was running through my head and the bartender was sitting down my wine glass, I felt a wave of warmth cover my entire being. It was like being drenched in the most perfect form of heat after sitting in a freezing hole all of my life.

"Hello Belle, I thought I would come and introduce myself. Is that ok?" The voice I knew even though we had not formally met. Its deep timbre mixed with velvety smoothness could not be denied. It was the singer, Christy's brother, of that, I was sure. When I turned around, I was proven correct and taken aback all at once. His eyes were the color of a darkened amber cognac, and his hair, which I thought was in a fade due to the shadows, was actually loc'd in some of the neatest manicured locs I have ever seen. They were edged up, braided, and hung down his back. I licked my lips from the pure deliciousness that was the man before me. When he stepped closer, I was sure that my ivory skin took on the color of crimson. I could not hide it. It is a not-so-wonderful consequence of being a light skin-colored black woman, and yes, I am all black.

His gaze covered my neck and then my face, as I am sure that is how the blush rose up my being. He gave me a lazy smile, and I ducked my head and took a deep breath.

He extended his hand and spoke again, "I'm Olivier LeBlanc, but my friends call me Dante."

I looked back up at him and saw the smirk playing on his lips. I finally got my wits about me, stopped staring, and shook his hand, "Elizabeth Monroe, my friends call me Liza."

"Well, Ms. Monroe, it is a pleasure to meet you." He smirked again.

I smiled and licked my lips. "Please call me Liza. Ms. Monroe is my mother."

"Fair enough." Then he leaned in and whispered close to my ear, "You are extremely captivating."

With him so close, I smelt the most intoxicating smell I have ever smelled. He smelled of wood, musk, and maple. It was warm and inviting, then fascinating and freeing all at once. I wanted to wrap myself in him and fall asleep. I leaned back slightly.

"I appreciate that......... You know, so are you, Mr. LeBlanc."

"Now, if I am to call you Liza since we are becoming friends, then you must call me Dante."

I leaned in ever so slightly, and a full smile spread across his lips. It was beautiful and enticing. Shoot, to be accurate, everything about him was inviting and enticing. There was only so much of this lust-driven coquettish conversation I could maintain. After all, my virgin senses were on full alarm. For the first time in my life, I think, no, I know, if this man asked me for my body, I would give it to him. Because as intoxicating as he was, his aura of sincerity and beauty made me believe I could trust him with me and my virginity.

All that being true, I was not one to back down in a conversation. So, I leaned in even further and whispered in his ear, "Now, who said we were becoming friends, Olivier."

He chuckled. It was the sound of a deep rumble like the thunder right before a storm. It stirred something completely sexual in me. He angled himself to be even closer to me and said, "Maybe, I would like to be friends. And let me be honest, none of my friends have made my name sound as amazing as it did coming from your lips just now."

With that, he leaned back and looked me in the eye. We were still closer than strangers should be, but it felt good. I know I was probably a shade of rosy pink like I had just run a race, but by the way, he kept looking at me, and with the sound of his voice so close to my ears, I think there was no other option but to let the blush stay and own it. So, I did. I stepped into his space and licked my lips, watching as his eyes followed the movement and his tongue mimicked mine. Then I smirked at him.

"I think you may need new friends then."

He roared in laughter, and I did the same. I took that moment to take a sip of my drink. He picked up the glass from the bartender. I guess when your parents are over the Club, your drink order is known. Oh wait, this was the guy whose parents were over the Order and who was my friend's brother, and I am just flirting with him like I am not trying to join this order. I looked into my glass and shook my head.

"Gurl, what are you thinking?" I said to myself. I must have said it out loud because Olivier leaned in and said, "You were being honest."

I looked up into those dark cognac-colored eyes, and I smiled. He was right. Plus, that was one of the reasons I was in New Orleans, to start living an honest life with myself. To really be me and stop letting other people tell me who I was or who I should be. So, I decided to own my honesty.

I raised my glass, and he followed suit, "To honesty."

"To honesty." We clinked our glasses and eyed each other as we took a sip.

At that moment, Christy decided to show up.

"Hey, how's it going? Oh, you met Dante. Are you being nice to her?"

He chuckled with a more brotherly sound than the one I heard at first and said, "Of course, aren't I always?"

"Huh, no. I'm surprised you are still here. You usually leave after your set. What's up?"

"The vote." He eyed me when he said that.

I shook my head. There was no way he was talking to me for a vote that I was sure of—virgin or not.

Christy put her hand on my shoulder, "Liza is great, right?"

"Yeah, I think she will fit just right." He cocked his head to the side. This guy is a real trip. I took some deep breaths because I knew I was about to start blushing, and apparently, so did he because his smile widened.

"Oh, my Gaud!! Liza, you ok?" Christy was looking at me, all worried. Yep, pretty sure I am turning red.

"Yeah, it's the alcohol. It goes to my head." Olivier and I started laughing.

Christy looked between the two of us for a few seconds.

"Are y'all drunk?"

"Oh, come on, Sis, you know I would never do that. At least not here."

"Right? And you?" She said, looking at me.

"Just nervous. You know, the vote and all. There are a lot of people here."

"You don't need to worry. You are doing great. I am hearing great things. Keep mingling. I have to go talk to someone." She turned to walk away. Then she turned back and, in a softer voice, stated, "Don't either of you think for a minute that I missed the sexual tension here." She pointed between us. "Dante, don't mess with her if you don't plan to stay, and Liza, be careful. This one will hurt you."

In unison, we said, "Noted."

"Good. Now have fun!! Mingle, Liza."

"I will."

With that, Christy walked away, and I finished my drink. Olivier just stayed and kept drinking slowly.

"Well, Olivier, it was a pleasure. I guess I should go mingle like a good candidate. Any suggestions?"

He looked at me from the side as he was facing the bar, "Be honest with yourself and with them. They are just regular people."

"Noted. See you around." I stood up straight after having been leaning against the bar.

"Yes, you most definitely will."

With that, he gave one of his beautiful smiles and wished me luck, and off I went to mingle.

Chapter 3: Liza

Back to one year ago

"So, how did everything work out with the Order?" Dr. Judy asked.

"It went well. I got accepted and eventually got initiated. I am still an active member. Truthfully at this point, I probably don't have a choice since Dante is my husband."

"How do you think the Order played in your relationship?"

"Well, that is a little complicated."

I start to think before I answer. I remember it took about six months before I was officially a member of the Chateau LeBlanc Chapter of the Order. The day I got inducted, we all received beautiful rose gold and titanium signet rings with an onyx gemstone behind the crest of the Order. I was so proud. It was the first thing I had done outside of my parents. The Order was terrific, from the community activity to the meetings that helped with personal and spiritual growth to career advancement opportunities to all the secrets we keep. I loved it. The more I learned, the more invested I became. It's crazy because none of my friends know about my membership or Dante's membership in the Order.

Back to the Order's role in our relationship being complicated. Okay, so I was inducted into the Order, and about three months later, I saw Olivier again. It was almost like he was purposely not around during the initiation period, or maybe Christy's warning rang true. I am not sure. Either way, I did not see him again until I was a sophomore. At this point, Christy and I had moved off campus and were staying in a high-rise condo that her parents were paying for. She was a senior and getting ready to graduate. Her goal was to go to Tulane and major in African American leadership and politics. I had never heard of such a master's program, but then again, I was only a sophomore. What did I know?

One day, I was leaving one of my chemistry classes, and I spotted Olivier across the campus. I had never seen him there before. Supposedly, from what Christy told me, he was an alumnus, and he was trying to figure out what he wanted to do with his life. Therefore, for now, he was just taking gigs singing and playing since he loved that. I watched as he talked with the Director of Campus Ministry. I knew her because I volunteered with them weekly. Anyway, he looked up during the conversation, and his eyes met mine, and he smiled genuinely. It warmed my heart. I wasn't sure why it warmed me so much, but it definitely did. He finished his conversation and began to walk toward me. I felt the butterflies swirling within me the closer he got.

However, by the time Olivier was halfway to me, my boyfriend Luke decided to come up and grab me from behind and spin me around. As I went flying, I saw the frown displayed on Olivier's face. I wanted to say sorry, but why. I mean, I did not owe him an explanation. Anyway, when Luke put me down facing him, he kissed me softly.

I met Luke during the initiation into the Order. We actually got inducted together. He was a great guy full of life and energy, and I really liked that. He was coffee-colored with a clean-shaven face and a neat fade, just the kind of guy I usually dated. He was pre-med and very knowledgeable. He was always attentive and caring with me like I was fragile and needed care. For some reason, everyone always assumed I needed care, except for my best friend from childhood, Lyric. She knew that I was still fun and exciting even though I was nerdy and quiet at times. She also knew that my quietness did not mean I was shy or that I needed to be protected.

Back to what happened. So, Luke put me down, and he kissed me. Of course, I kissed him back. I mean, he was my man, but it felt weird to know that Olivier was right behind us. I knew the moment Olivier made it to us because the sheer feel of his aura wrapped around me and made me want to turn around and run to him. I turned around slowly, and the frown was still slightly laying across his lips. I tilted my head to the side in confusion because, really, why was he frowning.

"Hey, Bro! What's up?" Luke dabbed Olivier up.

"Not much. Thought I would come by and speak with some people."

"You planning to come back and finish that pharm degree?"

That was news to me. As much as Christy had told me about her family, she had never told me that.

"Not going to happen. I need to figure out the next steps, though. I always seem to think better while walking on campus."

"I get that. Oh, I am sorry. You know my lady, Liza, right? We came through together."

Olivier gazed at me, "Of course." He stuck his hand out to me, "Ms. Monroe, it is a pleasure to see you again." He smirked.

I shook my head and then grabbed his hand. "Likewise, Olivier."

He chuckled that thunderous chuckle.

"Well, Dante, we were about to go out to eat. You want to come with us?"

I looked at Luke like he had lost his mind.

"Oh, come on, Babe. Dante is good people. We go way back."

"Fine," I stated reluctantly.

"Well, what you say, Bro?"

"That sounds great, actually."

I think my eyes almost popped out of my head. What is Olivier doing? I heard him chuckle to himself and my eyes narrowed.

We all started walking, and Luke told Olivier we were going to the Cheesecake Bistro, my favorite place to eat outside of the Club. The Club was where the Order was housed, and it had some of the most fantastic food. Luke's phone went off when we were about to part ways to go to our cars, and he excused himself.

"So, that is the kind of men you like?" Olivier said as soon as Luke was out of earshot. He stepped a little closer to me.

"Maybe. Is it something to you?" I countered.

"Maybe. You see, Elizabeth, I thought you had better taste than that." There was that smirk again. "I guess I was mistaken."

"We can't always have what we want, especially if it goes missing for months." I arched an eyebrow.

His mouth slightly dropped, and then he nodded his head up and down while licking his lips, "Noted, Belle. Noted."

He took some steps back as Luke came back around the corner. The truth was, I was happy Luke was coming back because I could not believe how forward I just was. I am not usually that forward.

"Hey, you guys. I am sorry, but I must cancel."

"Is everything ok?" I asked.

"Yeah, my Pops needs some help with his car ASAP. I am sorry, Babe. Hey, why don't you all still go, and then you can bounce questions about the Order off of Dante. I am sure he can answer all of them since he was born there." Luke chuckles and hits Olivier on his shoulder.

Olivier only smirked in response.

"I don't know..." I started.

"You know, he's right. If you have any questions, I am sure I know the answers. Plus, I did listen more than my sister when we had to attend meetings." Olivier offered.

I knew it was a bad idea for me to go out with him alone, but there was no way around it without it looking suspicious. I looked at Luke, and he was pleading because he knew I would be mad about missing my favorite cheesecake. Then I looked at Olivier, and he had this knowing look in his eye like he just knew I was going to agree. I narrowed my eyes at him, and he smiled full-on.

"Ok. Go ahead and take care of your Pops." I said. Luke kissed me and told me I was the best. Then, he told Olivier thanks and to take care of his girl, and then off he went. I stood there for a little bit before I looked at Olivier. When I did, I knew going out with Olivier would be the most beautiful mess I could get into.

Chapter 4: Liza

That one lunch was the beginning of my friendship with Olivier. As our friendship developed, I discovered that he was charming, funny, intelligent, and insightful, just as I thought he would be. We talked about every topic, from religion to politics to the future to sports. We would go to lunch, talk on the phone, and text throughout the day. It was truly unique. Interestingly, I noticed that the Olivier I spoke to and the Olivier who was at the Club or with his parents were completely different. With me, he was outgoing and talkative, always asking questions. With them, he was always silent and noncommittal unless it was truly necessary.

As I and Olivier's friendship grew and Christy and I got closer, I realized that the Order was so much a part of them and how they operated that anything outside of that was flawed. For instance, Christy originally wanted to get a master's in creative writing. However, that degree did not serve the Order, was what Christy said her mother told her.

Then when she said journalism, her mother said that the Order had enough of those. So, her current degree choice of African American leadership and politics is solely based on the Order's need to stay on top of what is going on in the community from a perspective other than a senator, congress member, military personnel, or future vice president. The Order already had those prospects in its pocket. When I tried to get her to explain more, she was like, that was just how things worked. I tried having the conversation with Olivier, and he just changed the subject.

I remember one evening when I was at the LeBlanc's house for dinner. We were all around the table. Monsieur LeBlanc was telling this funny story about what happened at Tulane, where he was a professor of Forensic Psychology and Behavioral Profiling. On this particular night, Olivier was late, which is not like him or any of the LeBlancs. So when he walked in about an hour late, and his father was in the middle of the story, everything stopped.

Lady LeBlanc, who is always dressed to kill, even when lounging at home, was dressed in a flowing satin maxi length dress that was copper in color. It truly went perfectly with her skin tone. The copper shimmered in the low light of the luxurious dining room and bounced off the mirrored wall.

Olivier came in looking tired and worn out but sexy all the same. He had on a pair of well-fitting ripped black ash jeans and a black sweater that looked as soft as his black beard. His mother approached him and hugged him close, and then she stepped back as if offended.

"So, Dante, you come to dinner late and then smell of smoke. I told you to stop smoking years ago. When did you restart?"

"Mother, please." Is all he said as he came to the table and sat across from me in his regular seat. I looked at Christy, and she just shrugged and went back to eating. Lady LeBlanc returned to the table and gave her husband the death stare as Olivier began to put food on his plate. It was crazy because it was like I was the only one watching things unfold.

Then Monsieur LeBlanc said, "Son, I am happy you could join us."

"Yeah."

"Have you gone back to smoking?"

"No."

Lady LeBlanc huffed at Olivier's response.

"Well, Son, is there something you would like to share, like why you were late and smell of smoke?"

"No."

"Dante, please meet me halfway." Monsieur LeBlanc pleaded. At that, Olivier lifted his eyes, and for the first time that evening, his eyes met mine. They were dark and sad, something I had not noticed before. He blinked and the sadness was gone. Then he looked at his father. Was I imagining things?

"Okay, I was at Club Envoy. Tonight was cigar night hence the smell of smoke. I forgot to bring a change of clothes, or I would have changed." He said it so matter of fact, with no inflections or feelings. It was like watching someone else. Then, when Lady LeBlanc responded, I realized why.

"So, you are singing at a Club, and a Club by a rival Order at that. Dante, are you crazy!" Lady LeBlanc scolded. It was the first time in over a year of attending dinner at their house that I had heard her raise her voice. It was intimidating. But Olivier didn't flinch. He just went back to eating.

"Son, what your mother is saying, is why that Club? We know you are trying to get this music feeling out of your system, but why go to a rival?" His dad tried to put a little sugar on the questions, but it was no use. Olivier was not here for it. He stood up and drank his water and then started for the door.

"Oh, no," I heard Christy whisper. I looked her way, and she motioned for me to keep my head down. *What*? Was the thought going through my head.

"Oh, so you come home to disrespect us with your smell and timing, and now you are going to just leave. We taught you better than this, Olivier." His mother screamed at him.

"Sweetheart, let's take a moment. We do have company."

"Liza is basically family. So, Olivier, you are just going to leave?" At this point, Olivier was almost at the front door, which you could see as it was a straight walk from where we were past the living room to the door. He put his hand on the door.

"Son, please let's talk about this. You cannot keep living your life this way. There are only so many times we can cover for you at the Order. Please tell me how we can help. What is going on?"

At this point, Christy was looking between her brother and parents. When she saw that Olivier was turning the knob, she said to her parents, "Just let him go. That is what he does anyway. Right, Dante, run from your problems. Yeah, we see how well that has worked for you."

To say I was shocked at Christy's statements was an understatement. I had never heard her speak to her brother with such disdain. It almost sounded like she hated him or something.

At Christy's word, Olivier turned around. The look of pure hurt that crossed his handsome features broke my heart. He looked devastated. As he walked back into the room, his eyes were solely on Christy's. As he approached, his whole being commanded respect. He held more power in his walk and eyes than I had ever seen. He stopped in front of Christy's chair, and she rose. They stared each other down— each one waiting on the other to break.

"Children, please let us talk this through." Neither of them acknowledged their father's request.

Finally, Olivier let his head hang, and he shook his head in disbelief.

His voice was wounded and broken, "Christy, I expect this from them but not you. I thought we had each other's back."

"How can I have your back if you don't even talk to me anymore?"

"I talk...," He trailed off and took a deep breath. "You are becoming more and more like them. You no longer understand or try to understand."

"Because you are being selfish. Our family has built this Order for generations. We cannot just turn our backs on it."

"No one is saying that."

"But your actions speak more than your words, Dante."

"Christy is right. You cannot say you support this family, but you won't choose a career but instead frolic around like a broke musician." At Lady LeBlanc's words, Olivier took some steps back as if he had just been wounded. I have to admit, I felt injured for him.

Then I saw when the change in him happened. He stood up all the way. He straightened out his shoulders and rolled them back. He narrowed his eyes and spoke with sure clarity and masculinity, "This is the problem right here. You all think that my life should be run by an Order I had no choice but to be a part of. I love you all, and I love the Order, but what I will not do is live for a group of people who only seek to hold more and more power. I want to live my life and enjoy it. I am not frolicking around like a broke musician. I am being invited and highly sought after to sing and perform all over the city and state, shoot even the country. And you know what? I cannot share that with my family because you will not congratulate me and allow me to take this journey. No, you will shun me for going against the grain." He turned to Christy. "You once understood my quest, but now you are just like them. To be honest, I do not fault you. I saw it coming, but I will not let you or any of you make me feel like I have done something wrong by following my heart. Is this my career path? No. Is it my now, though? Yes. You guys have a nice dinner. I am no longer hungry." Then he looked at me. "Sorry, you had to be here for this." With that, he walked out of the house. We all sat there in silence for a while. Christy eventually sat down, and we finished our dinner in silence.

When we left her parent's house and were driving back home, Christy started crying.

"Christy, it will be ok," I tried to comfort her.

"I have never seen him that angry before. I messed up. I mean, I have been thinking those things for a while, but I did not mean to say them." We pulled into our parking spot at the condo, and she looked at me. "I love my brother, and he is the smartest man I know. But he chose to waste it on a career he doesn't even want."

"Christy, is it possible he is trying to figure out what he really wants as he says?"

"No." She starts shaking her head. "He has always known he wanted to be a custom instrument maker. It has been his dream from birth. Well, you know what I mean. But he refuses just to say that and fight for that. Instead, he acted like he wanted to be a pharmacist to appease them and now he acts like her wants to entertain."

I didn't really know what to say to that. So, I just hugged her, and we eventually went inside.

As I got ready for bed, I thought about the events of the night, and I felt terrible for Olivier. He was alone. When I finished my bedtime routine, I got in bed and pulled out my phone. I decided to text him.

You ok?

There was a long pause. I put the phone down and waited. It was a little after 1am. He could be sleeping. Then my phone beeped.

U want me to be honest?

Yes

No Im not.

Where r u?

The W Hotel on Poydras

I stopped to think. *Really why did I ask him that?* Apart of me wanted to ask, if he needed company? The other part of me was confused, really. Before I could figure out what I wanted to say, He continued.

Don't you have class in the morning?

Yeah at 7:50a. I have a lab.

Then?

English. Then I am done. It will be about 1p. What do you have tomorrow?

Do you want to come to my gig tomorrow?

The elusive standing Friday night gig?

Don't be dramatic Liza.

Yes, I would love to.

He took a minute, then replied.

Thank you.

For?

Being interested to see what I do. Everyone else blows me off.

I heard. Sorry about that.

Yeah, well such is life.

Not always.

Always the optimist.

Only when you are the pessimist.

Not pessimist, just realist.

Ok, Mr. Realist. I should go to sleep. I will see you tomorrow.

Tomorrow then. Goodnight.

Goodnight.

With that, I put down my phone, and I went to sleep dreaming of Olivier.

The next day when I was leaving English, I saw Luke in the front of the Admin Building talking to some people. I decided to go the other way. The truth is, for the past two months or so, I started dodging him. I don't really know why. Technically, he is still my boyfriend, but I am just not interested in getting to know him anymore. I do not know, but I definitely need to figure out why I am no longer interested. Hopefully, I figure it out before I need to break up with him. More than likely, it is just me having so much to do with school, community service, and the Order's many events. I really just don't have time for him. Let's not forget church. Maybe that was it. He invited me to church, and his church was beyond weird. After that, I started pulling away. I don't know. I shake my head to get rid of my thoughts as I pass the freshman dorms. But just when I think I made it, I hear.

"Babe!!......Liza! Hold up!"

I turn around. He was too close for me to play like I didn't hear him.

"Hey, you," I say and step into his arms for a quick hug.

"So, I was thinking. Winter Break is coming, and my family always hosts a holiday party. This year, it is the day of the Order's Holiday Bash. Would you be my date to the party?" He asked sweetly.

I play dumb, though. "Luke, I will already be at the Holiday Bash, doing community service in both places and the party after."

"Liza, you know I meant my family's party, not the bash." He laughs and pulls me closer. I want to say no. It must be written on my face because he says, "Babe, do you not want to meet my family? We have been dating for over a year now."

"Luke, it's not that. It is just...." I trail off because it is that and then some. Then I realize precisely what the then some is, as I get distracted looking at the man getting out of his ocean blue Tundra Sport. The man is wrapped in bleached-out black jeans, a black and teal shirt with a nice afro-centric/tribal vibe, and some black Tims, not tied, were on his feet. His locs hung freely down his back and around his shoulders. I watched as he pulled his locs into a loose ponytail and slid on some aviators and a black jacket. Olivier was Fine!!

"Liza, are you listening to me?" The frustration coming from Luke's voice pulled me out of my examination of Olivier just as Olivier noticed me and sent me a nod. Luke must have turned around because when I finally looked Luke's way, he was looking at Olivier. "So, is he why you have been pushing me away?"

"What? No. Of course not." I say, focusing back on the conversation we were having.

"You sure because you always seem to get distracted when he is around. Ever since you guys went to lunch without me that time."

"Luke, don't make it sound that way. You told us to go. You basically pushed me to go to lunch without you."

"Oh. So, you are saying I pushed you into the arms of another man. A Brother at that. Where is your honor, Liza? Have you learned nothing from the Order?"

I was taken aback by the audacity of this dude. "First of all, Olivier and I are friends, which you are well aware of. His sister is my friend and roommate. Second of all, my honor? Have I learned nothing? Understand something, Luke Covington. The Order did not give me honor. I came to New Orleans with it, and furthermore, the gall of you to question my honor when you spend so much time kissing the asses of anybody who may be of use to you later, from professors to pastors to members of the Order. I do not know how you have any dignity or honor left. The audacity of you to question my honor." By the time I was done talking, I was all in his face. Well, as much as my 5'8" frame would allow me to get in the face of someone who was 6'3". He was staring at me with such disdain I was sure he was about to let me have it.

He leaned down to get into my face and whispered, "Liza, you have no idea who you are, let alone how to honor yourself or anyone else. You think you know, but you have no clue how this world works. You just burned the best bridge you had. Don't worry about the party or anything else for that matter. I don't need a woman who cannot see the man standing in front of her because she is too busy looking at what is not hers. We are done." With that, he walked away and left me looking after his back. I don't know how long I was standing there, and I knew people were looking at me. After all, I was standing in the middle of the path. The truth is, I couldn't move because he was right on so many accounts.

"Hey, Belle. You good?" I heard Olivier ask and felt his warm hand on my shoulder. He turned my chin to him when I did not answer. "Liza, do I need to go handle him?" He examined my face. I shook my head. Then I met his eyes. They were filled with concern. "Belle, then what?"

"He broke up with me. He said I don't know who I am and I have no honor, and I couldn't see him because I was too busy looking at what didn't belong to me."

"I'm sorry what? Was he calling you a hoe?" Olivier was looking around for Luke now. I could feel the anger rolling off of him.

"No. He was saying." I took a breath. Then I met Olivier's eyes through his shades, "He was saying I was too busy looking at you." I saw the weight of my admission as it became clear in his mind, and then I looked away. I don't know what I expected from Olivier at that moment, but what happened was not it. He pulled me into him and hugged me in the middle of the path. It was warm and intoxicating, just like his scent when it wrapped around me. I hugged him back.

Then he whispered, "You distract me too, Belle." I looked up and saw his smirk, and I smiled. "Come on, Belle, let's get something to eat." He grabbed my hand and started walking.

When we got to the car, and he opened my door, before I got in, I said, "Wait isn't this against the Order's rules somehow? Something about your Brother's ex something?"

Olivier smiled that killer watt smile I loved so much, "The rule you are talking about applies to your Brother's ex-wife, not his girlfriend, and the rule is about dating. Plus, I tend to break many of those rules when it comes to you, Belle."

A look of pure shock covered my face. What other rules had he broken pertaining to me?

"Stop thinking. I will not tell you. Just get in. I am hungry, and I know you are too." I stared at him a moment longer, and he smirked at me. Then I finally slid into the truck. He closed my door and walked around.

Man, there is so much I obviously don't know. I guess Luke was right about that too.

Chapter 5: Olivier, aka Dante

Back to one year ago

"Dr. Judy, I do not understand the point of going back that far in our relationship. We have been seeing you for some time and have moved passed many a thing. What exactly are we doing here?" I asked the good doctor. Dr. Judy has been our marriage counselor for a little bit now, and she has helped us move on and be the better couple that we are. In fact, I am trying to understand why Liza is so insistent we are not done with therapy altogether. Our marriage is better than it has been in a while. She even stopped calling me Dante. I am ok with everyone else calling me that, but Liza, no. To Liza, I have always been Olivier, and when she calls me Dante, it is like she called me out of my name.

"To be frank, Dante, you guys have moved passed many things, but I realized you guys have dealt with nothing. The two of you seem to be on a busy stream, trying to get to the next thing and not being honest with anything if it will cause a delay."

"Dr. Judy, that is not true. We dealt with many things since we have been here, right Olivier?" Liza looks to me to confirm. I look into my wife's eyes, and then I pause. For the first time in a long time, I take a good look at what her eyes are saying that she is not. We used to always read each other. It is one of the reasons that our bond was so deep. We could see what the other was hiding from the world, and the other couldn't help but divulge. Somewhere along the line, we stopped. We stopped being honest with ourselves and each other. I can tell she feels me searching her inner thoughts because she begins to move in her seat. She eventually diverts her eyes, and that is when I say, "Sorry, Belle, I can't say that we have. Dr. Judy is right."

She looks back at me as if I have just betrayed her, but then I gaze into her eyes long enough for the realization that we are both right to take root. She sighs and looks away. "Fine, so we tend to move past things and not bring them up again. It works for us. Is that so bad?" She looks at our therapist with hope. I already know the answer to that.

"Liza, that is a problem. It means you are not getting to the bottom of the issue. You are simply continuing a cycle that does not serve either of you."

Liza goes to say something again. I put a hand up as if I am about to touch her leg, but I see her flinch. So, I stop, and she contains whatever she is about to say. I put my hand back in my lap and take a deep breath. Therapy is always so hard. "Doctor, what do you suggest we do?"

"Continue with where we are. Dante, do you think that you have broken the Order's rules when it comes to Liza?"

I hear Liza's sharp intake of breath. I run my tongue across my teeth, mouth closed, of course. It is a bad habit I have when people ask me questions I would rather not answer. However, answer I do, "Yes."

"A lot of them?"

"Yes."

"Can you expound?"

"Ok."

As I think about it, the truth is, the day I met Liza, I broke the rules. My parents agreed to my singing career, however short, as long as I promised to marry the girl of their choosing and not fraternize with anyone from the Order.

The idea was that if I was going to be a musician, I was obviously going to be sleeping around. These were my parent's thoughts. Honestly, though, I didn't need to sing to get those kinds of offers. Nonetheless, I agreed not to fraternize with anyone from the Order, but I would choose my own wife and allow them an opinion. They took the deal.

However, when I saw Liza walk into that candidate appraisal party, I could not keep my eyes off her. From the beautiful black hair that she had in a neat updo to the smoothness of her skin to the length of her neck to the faint hint of curves beneath her dress to those fantastic legs in heels. She looked gorgeous, and I wanted a closer look. Going up to her at the bar would have passed if I had kept my distance, but I was a goner once I saw the twinkle in her green hazel eyes and her plump pink lips. She gave as good as she got in the wit and flirting department, and I enjoyed every second of it. When she leaned in to whisper to me, I had never smelt anyone as heavenly and erotic as she. She smelled of rose and sandalwood. An amazing mixture that made me want to grab her. I struggled to keep my hands to myself.

That exchange that night was broken rule #1. It got me in a world of trouble with my parents. They reminded me of my promise and told me to stay clear, and I did until I saw her at Xavier. The fact that Luke was her boyfriend was maddening. I knew Luke from childhood, and, truthfully, he was a good guy, but not for Liza. Liza was a treasure, a rare beauty that deserved to be taken care of by me. It was crazy when I realized why it angered me so. I wanted her. So, I befriended her, broken rule #2.

Christy always made me stay away from her friends, but I never had to chase them. Eventually, they came to me, not Liza, though. After the lunch we had alone due to Luke's cancelation, I had to go over to their apartment and go to family dinner regularly just to see her at first. Then she started accepting my text and calls. We became friends. Really good friends, actually. I was not the kind of guy who had many female friends, so being so close to Liza was interesting. The first time I invited her to one of my gigs, and she came, I think that is when I fell in love with her.

The invitation to a gig was broken rule #3, and falling in love with her was #4. The Order had a rule against marrying someone in the Order. The idea was, that it was best for one's spouse to be unaware because of all the things that happened behind closed doors. My parents actually were from different chapters of the Order and met in college.

That was ok, but being from the same chapter was forbidden. The thing is, women know part of the secrets, and men know the other part. A couple could put all of the pieces together and find where all of the dead bodies lay. Different chapters tend to hold various pieces. This is why dating and marrying someone from another chapter was okay. So, falling in love with Liza was a problem for the Order, but my love was my secret at first.

The first gig I invited her to was at Club Virtue. One of the most crowd-pleasing clubs I gigged. Club Virtue was decorated in deep greens and dark grays. When the lights hit the colored glass ceiling, it made the place look mysterious and alluring. That night I had a car pick Liza up and bring her to the club since I had to be there before the club opened. I was setting up for my gig as the previous performer had just left. I was adjusting my mic, and in she walked. She had on one of those dresses that fit like a second skin. I could see every curve she had, from the swell of her breast to the round curve of her hips to her shapely legs ending at the sparkling shoes on her feet. She had her hair down, and the curls were everywhere. She had on no glasses, something I had never seen her go without, and she was mesmerizing. Her diamond hoop earrings seemed to make her eyes sparkle. When she finally noticed I was on stage, she offered me a slight wave, and I smiled. I nodded my head toward the VIP section, which was the club's lounge area that they let performers use when they were done with their set. She walked into the area just as I began to sing. I would catch her eye during every song, and she would be grooving to the music, from the fast songs that make you jump to the slow songs that make you grind. When I started singing one of Tank's oldies, I looked her way and saw how she swung her hips in that slow whine which had me wanting to be right behind her.

After finishing my set, I thanked my crew and headed her way. She was talking to one of the ladies in the section. When I walked up, her eyes twinkled, and she smiled one of those smiles that reached her eyes. She excused herself and walked up to me slowly, then she leaned in with her hand on my chest and said in my ear, "You did amazing tonight. I love the variety."

I licked my lips and said, "What about the last song?"

She took a sip of her drink, then she smirked at me, "I had never heard that last song before, but I think I liked it best. It made me miss home with all that bass, and the words made me want to find someone to share a dance with." When she said that last part, she grinded on me from the side, then tried to back away. I pulled her closer, this time to the front instead of the side of me.

"Liza, you look beautiful tonight," I spoke into her ear.

She turned red, something I found cute, but I would never tell her. "Dante..."

"Olivier," I corrected her.

"Olivier, thank you. Your song was exquisite."

"How do you know it was mine?"

"Because of the way you sang it. It was like you felt every last note. It was breathtaking."

I smiled. "Dance with me, Belle."

"Absolutely."

We danced until Club Virtue closed and then walked the French Quarter. She put her hand in the nook of my arm, and I brought her in close, and we just walked and talked until the sun came up.

Chapter 6: Olivier

Back to one year ago

"Do you still break the rules for her?" Dr. Judy asks.

"No."

"Why not?"

I looked at Liza, and she wouldn't look at me.

"She considered aborting my baby." My voice cracked. Then she looked at me. Liza knew what I would say. I saw the tears in her eyes. Then I felt the wetness on my cheek. I looked away from her and wiped my tears away.

"Dante, I was just thinking about my options."

"Options you were considering without me. Liza, it would have been different if this was the first time, but it was not. After the first time, we said we would always talk things through together, and you didn't."

"Oh, like you talked things through when you decided to move us to Houston to finally start a career."

"That was different, and you know it."

"Just let it go."

"No, don't let it go. Keep talking. Follow it through." The therapist encouraged.

"Fine. No, it is not different. You made us move because it was the best thing for you. You did not think about us." Liza continued.

"I didn't think about us? All I ever do is think about us. I moved us to Houston because your family is here. I could have moved us to New York; that would have been better for me."

"You still could have had a conversation with me and not just made choices that would affect me and the kids without my knowledge."

She was crying now, and all I wanted to do was comfort her, but it was no use. She would not let me touch her. I didn't say anything, just stared and shook my head.

"What are you thinking, Dante?" Dr. Judy said.

"About what?"

With that response, Liza let out a huff and crossed her arms over her chest.

"About everything your wife just said?" Dr. Judy added.

I took a moment and then replied, "She is right."

Liza's head snapped back my way.

"Expound, please. And to your wife."

"Liza, I should have talked to you about finally opening my custom instrument business. I should have talked to you about moving." I gaze into her eyes. She is not sure if she believes my apology. I can see it in her eyes.

"Why didn't you, Dante?" Liza asks.

"Honestly?"

"Yes."

"Because I didn't want you to say no. I knew you were finishing up your latest formula, and then you would have a break. I figured that would be the best time. You were pregnant with our second child. I needed to get a move on what I was doing before it was no longer a thing."

"So, you just decided?"

"Yes."

"I would have agreed, Olivier. I would have gone anywhere with you. We were in Atlanta because of you." She put her head down. I reached out for her leg again, and she moved away.

"What about you? How could you consider aborting my baby a second time, huh?"

She spoke lowly, "I didn't want any more children."

"That is what you said the last time."

"It's the truth."

"Is it the only truth?" I challenged. My voice was rising.

"Fine. No, it is not. The rest is simple. I was not sure if I still wanted to be married. I was feeling like I was drowning already. I did not want to bring another child into all of that."

After a long silence between us, the therapist asks, "Why did you have the baby, Liza?"

"Because I love my husband, and I knew he would never forgive me otherwise."

"Wait, so you still don't want Sydney?" I was becoming frantic. Is she serious right now? Could she really be sitting here and saying that she still does not want our beautiful little girl?

"I did want her by the time of delivery, but for a little over half of my pregnancy, I didn't."

I sighed and put my hands on my head. What happened to us? We were so in love, and now we are talking about her not wanting our fourth child.

"Olivier, please hear me. I love you and what we have, but I wanted to figure myself out and get my career going. I can't do that if I am always barefoot and pregnant."

"Liza, you have a booming chemistry career. Every major cosmetic company in the world wants to recruit you. So, try again with that career stuff."

"Fine. I was drowning. I didn't know who I was anymore. I figured another kid would only add to my confused state."

"Why didn't you just say that?"

"Because how could I do that when you are always busy?"

"Liza, I am never too busy for you or the kids."

"Except for Monday through Friday when you have work to do. Oh, let's not forget, every 2nd and 4th Saturday for the Order." Liza yelled.

"Ok, let us take a breather. You guys need to remember you still love each other, which means there is still hope." Dr. Judy interjects. With that, Dr. Judy said we should take a 5-minute break, and then she walked out of the counseling room and probably went to her office. The room we do therapy in is called the therapy room and, therefore, not her office.

After Dr. Judy walks out, Liza stands up and goes to the window. She stares out of it, looking at the beautiful lake in view. I stare at her. I look at how her shoulders droop and how her once naturally curly hair, which used to be worn so freely, is now straight and down her back. I look at how her once lean frame with slight curves has filled out to become the thick woman with delicious curves that stands before me. It was like with each child we had, the more I saw her body change into the beautiful woman that is my wife today. However, I think the curves and thickness that I love on her, and the stretch marks that are the evidence of our love producing a child within her, do not bring her the same pride and seductiveness that I feel when I look at her. From the corner of my eye, on many occasions, I have watched as she looked at herself as if she did not like what she saw, watched her suck in her stomach, and critically pull at the meat on her thighs. I try to compliment her, but she does not believe me, and I have nothing. I mean, I don't know what to do with her unbelief. So now I watch this woman I love, but I am not sure I know her anymore. It's not that I think we have grown apart, but more so unclear about the other's wants and desires. I don't think she wants to leave, but I do not know. I am at a loss. The state I seem to always be in with her as of late.

I lean forward, put my head in my hands, and allow my fingers to massage my scalp. We stay in the same position for a while, not saying anything, just lost in our own collective thoughts. Then I finally have had enough.

"Liza, why are we here?" I ask, looking up at her frame still facing the window.

She doesn't look at me. "Because I need us to be."

"But why?"

"It is an intensive. A one-day intensive with someone who has counseled us for a while."

"Liza, but why do we need to be here? I understand you need it. That is why I am here because you asked. But you have yet to explain what you want us to get from this. Right now, it is doing us more harm than good."

"You know, it is always worse before it gets better. This is not our first rodeo." She says but still not looking at me.

"That's the problem, Liza. It's not. We continue to visit the same things and continue to not deal with our issues. You continue to hold on to what really makes you want to come and then act like you are happy when you are not. Liza, I love you, but I need you to talk to me."

"You used to be able to read me."

I take a long deep breath and stand and start to pace. I take another long deep breath hoping it will ease the tension rallying inside of me. I realize as I begin to talk it did not work. "Yeah, that is before you shut me out."

She turns at my tone. She stares at me long and hard. "Dante, so, are we finally going to do this? Have the conversation about what happened?"

I turn away from her and grit my teeth. It is no use. I feel myself bubbling up on the inside. I feel my anger and my disappointment. I feel the wall I secured tightly inside crumbling. The wall that I know was intended, so this conversation never happened. When I turn around and see the look of disgust and hurt in her eyes, I know we need to do this. I let the wall crumble. I feel my shoulders fall, and then I take a long breath and say, "I guess so."

She stares at me, shocked that I am willing. "Do you want me to start?" She asks.

"Sure. Ladies, first," I say as I sit. I feel defeated, and we have not even started.

"Dante," I cringe at the sound of the name rolling off her tongue. I literally feel my body cringe, and I know she sees it because she stops talking. There is silence, and then I look up at her, and she stares at me with tears in her eyes. She refuses to let them fall. I watch as she hides from me by turning around and collecting herself before she starts again.

"I went to the clinic for information. You were never supposed to know that I went there. I did not want to kill our baby. I just needed to know that I had options. I no longer felt like I had options in anything. My job was not what I thought it was anymore. People just wanted to make money and didn't care what was in the products. They wanted to lie to customers and call things vegan and clean when it was anything but. Then I would come home, and instead of refuge, I would be bombarded by everyone's else needs. I stopped feeling reprieved by going to see the girls for brunch for our Label Ladies' outings. I couldn't talk to you because you were busy building and growing the business. You had started being more active in the Order, which I was happy about, but that left me to tend to 3 kids alone when I was already so drained. I hated how I looked and how I felt in my own body. Then I found out I was pregnant, and I honestly wanted to die. I didn't think I had anything left to give. After Lex was born, I had such bad postpartum depression I could not endure that again. I felt hopeless and alone, even though people surrounded me. After I had Sydney, I felt worse. I thought we were better, but I felt more and more of myself slipping away on the inside. Not in that, you are growing for the better kind of way, but in that, you are melting away into nothingness kind of way. I tried talking to each of our mothers, but our moms were no use. They keep pushing me to keep going. But on the inside, I just needed to stop and think, stop and figure myself out. Everything about our lives is scheduled. Nothing is fun or spontaneous. There are calendars and calendars of things from kids' events to your work events to my work events and projects. I practically schedule when I will take a pee break every day. There is no time left for me to be me. Our house does not even reflect me. There is no haven for me anywhere." She is bent over crying, and I want to go to her, but I also know she needs to get this out. So, I sit on the couch and watch my wife fall apart, and as she breaks, so does my heart. She has taken a pause and is breathing slowly and deeply like she is trying to calm the raging storm within. I stare at her. She is my heart. My world, and she is broken on my watch. But then, so am I. What am I to do?

Then she continues with her back to me, "I stole away to that Mini Poweress Retreat because I felt like if I didn't, I would not survive. I was ending." She turns around and meets my eyes. "I am not saying I was going to kill myself. I am saying I needed reprieve, and I didn't know what else to do. So, I went, and what I learned and what made me ask you to come here with me is because I realized I didn't know myself. Somewhere along the way, I have lost sight of my identity. I no longer know who I am as Liza. My identity is washed into being all the roles I play, but that is what I do. It is who I am for others. But who am I for me, and who am I when I am not picking up toys and dropping off kids, making new lipsticks, and making new lashes." She stops and looks down, the tears start flowing again, and her voice cracks, "who am I when……I am not trying to be your wife, but I am just your wife. I don't know who she is anymore." I am at her side before she finishes.

I tentatively take her hand in mine, and she doesn't flinch. She lets me. She looks up at me with tears still streaming down her beautiful face but a small smile of appreciation is on her lips for me coming to her aid. After looking at our joined hands, she continues, "Then Trina said to me at the retreat, maybe I needed to stop hoping for the old me and figure out who the new me is. Who is this woman? This woman who has all the degrees, who has four children, and who is married to you. Who is she? So, that is why we are here. I lost me, and I don't know where I lost me or how to find me." She removes her hand from mine and walks to the other side of the room.

I take a deep breath. This distance between us is killing me. However, I do not move. Instead, I ask, "And what else?"

She looks at me. "You mean my feelings about finding you alone in the office jacking off to porn because you no longer sleep with me after Syndey was born? Is that the what else you mean?"

I swallow. "Yes."

"Why don't you start with the cruelty of the argument when you found me at the clinic?"

"Liza, I am sorry that you feel like you have lost yourself. I am sorry that nothing I have done helped you not lose you. I am sorry that you do not see the beautiful woman that I see." She says nothing, just takes her gaze away from me, and starts to pace. It is my turn to go look out the window. I watch as the fountain sprays water, and I think back to the argument she just brought up. It was nasty and went way too far. We never talked about it later just went on like nothing happened, which was a mistake.

"Liza, I was angry. I thought you had gone in there and killed our baby. I thought you had just had an abortion, and you didn't even talk to me. I was angry."

"And that makes it ok for you to call your wife a selfish bitch, Dante?" She screams.

I turn and look at her. I walk up to her. "No. No. It doesn't. Liza, I am sorry for calling you out of your name. I am sorry for saying that you had no right to make choices about our future without talking to me when I had taken the same liberties. I am sorry that, along the way, I have become this dictator. It is not who I am. Belle, I am sorry." I held her gaze in my eyes as she searched to determine my sincerity. The truth is, I had thought about that argument a lot, and as much as my anger was justified, my word choice was not. That I knew. But I was not the only one to blame, and that I needed her to admit to.

She finally nodded. "I am sorry, I let you believe that I had had an abortion. It was wrong of me. I should have talked to you about how I felt when I found out I was pregnant. I should have talked to you before I went to that clinic. You finding me there should not have happened because I should have talked to you first. We should have figured out what was best together. I am sorry." She looked away. But still stayed close.

I stepped into her space a little more, and she did not move. "About the office," I start as she brings her gaze back to mine. "When you had Syndey, and the postpartum depression came back.....I felt helpless." It was my turn to turn around and walk away. I started to pace. "I never told you, but the first time you had postpartum depression, it was devastating on me too. I did my best to take care of the kids and push as many things off my plate so that I could be there for you and the kids. I ended up putting my business on hold. It was not the developer that said the building was not clear to build. It was me. I stopped it. There was no way I could do that and be there for you. So, I chose."

I felt her eyes on me, but I did not look at her. I never intended to say any of what I was saying or about to say. I was never going to tell her. I continued all the same. "I took the money I was using for the business and used it to take care of us, which lasted until your depression was resolved and you went back to work. The problem was the rest of the money I had was wrapped up in the Order, which meant for me to get money for the business and us, I had to return to the Order. As much as I didn't want to do that, we needed it. So, I did." I shrugged and looked out the window. "To return to the Order and receive my due funds, I had to take my official rank and officiate the way I was supposed to. So, again, I did. When the postpartum came back, the good part was the doctor knew how to resolve it quickly, but the bad part was it brought back all the memories for you and me. It was at that time that the Order decided to take in new candidates, and with the chapter in Houston not having done so before, they needed Dad and me to officiate. I wanted to decline due to our new baby and what was happening with you, but I couldn't. I was under obligation, and to break such obligation would backfire in ways I did not want for either of us. So, I went. You were angry, and I was too. Eventually, I began to blame you for me having to participate in the foolery and give my time in a way I did not want. I started to resent you. So, even when you felt better and some time had passed, I was not interested in being intimate with you because I blamed you."

I turned around and looked into her eyes. I could read the shock and the horror. "Liza, I know it was not fair of me to blame you or take it out on you. For that, I am sorry. I should have talked to you, but I thought I was doing what I needed to do to take care of you and our kids."

I turned away. "Of course, me not being intimate with you did not take away the urge. So, I ended up watching porn and handling my needs on my own." I turned and looked at her. "You found me in the office doing just that, and I know you wanted to ask me questions. But we did what we always do, which is move on as if nothing happened, and that did not help us. After all, here we are." I turn around and walk up to her, walking into her space just a little. She stays. "Belle, just ask me the questions. Whatever you are thinking is playing out in our marriage, whether you say it or not. We need to be honest. I get that you need to find yourself, and I am on board with giving you time and me time to do that but worrying about me and what I am doing will not help you. Just ask me, Belle."

She holds my gaze for a long moment. She presses those naturally pink lips together and then blows out a breath. I can tell she is deciding whether she really wants and needs to know the answers to her questions. Then she decides. "How long have you been watching porn?"

I smirk. "Since I was 13 years old. Off and on," I say, trying to lighten the tension she has built up.

"You know what I mean." She smirks back and takes a swallow. Her vibe is lighter, not as light as I would like, though.

"Honestly, I started watching it a little more regularly after Sydney was three years old."

"What do you mean regularly?"

"Honestly?"

"Yes."

"2-3 times a week. I don't need it to handle my business, Liza. It is just entertaining."

"Do you..." She looks down. Then she looks back up at me. "Do you ever think about me?"

I smile broadly. "All the time. I think about all parts of you, Liza. From your mouth to your full breast, to those thick thighs, to that nice ass, to those long legs of yours. I think about all of you, Liza. All the time."

She turns red, that cute tent I love to see play across her skin. It tells me I said something extraordinary even though she will not say it aloud. She takes a deep breath and then steps back. She walks to the window. Here comes her real question. The one that has her flinching when I touch her.

She looks at me. Holding my gaze, she says, "Did you cheat on me after Sydney was born?"

I close the distance she has put between us. I stand in her space. So much so, she leans into the window. I want to make sure she sees me clearly when I answer her. "That is not your real question, Liza. Ask me the real question."

She looks down and shakes her head. "I am not sure I want to know that answer."

I use my finger, and I lift her chin until her eyes meet mine. She doesn't flinch. When her eyes are on mine, I peer into her eyes the way I used to. I look for the pieces she is choosing not to say, and I allow her to gaze at me in that way that gives her the truth of my soul and the keys to my heart. Since the first night, she came to my gig, I have been hers and that has not changed. I let her see that as she peers at me. She finally takes a deep breath and says, "Have you ever cheated on me?"

"No, Belle. I have never cheated on you. Not before Syndey was born or after she was born. All I want is you."

"Do you still resent me?"

I take a deep breath. I shake my head and say, "No, I don't. I made a choice. I just need to change it. I love the Order, but I don't want it to be this much a part of our lives again. It is not you I blame. It is me." I take a step back and let my head fall as I think about what changes I need to make. She takes a moment and watches me, then she walks into my space and lifts my chin so that our eyes meet. She gently touches my chest, leans in, and says, "Don't blame yourself or me. You did what was needed, and I thank you for being the head of our house and taking care of us. We missed, and we lacked nothing because of the sacrifice you made. We will figure out how to remove ourselves from the Order so that we are not as involved, but please, no more blame. Promise me."

Within her eyes, I see the woman I fell in love with. I hear her. She may not know who she is, but I do. I see her. "I will promise to stop blaming if you promise to let me help you find you. Because I see you."

I hold out my hand, and she shakes it, "I promise......I will let you help me."

"Let us also agree that we will stop letting things go by as if nothing happened and that we will talk things out with each other," I say.

"I agree wholeheartedly, Olivier."

I look into her eyes. She has not said my name in that tone with that look in so long.

"Please, say it again."

She smiles. "Olivier." I smile at her.

As we are smiling at each other, Dr. Judy comes back in.

"Well, it looks like we are ready for part 3 of this intensive."

We sit on the couch, and it dawns on me that she has been gone a while.

"Dr. Judy, that was more than 5 minutes. You left us in here like that on purpose. Didn't you?"

"Did it work?"

Liza shakes her head and chuckles. I smirk. "Yeah, it worked. We are talking. Now what?"

"Now we figure out how to get you back to being happily married. Sometimes you need to have the tough conversations so you can get down to what you both really need and want out of this marriage. Are you guys ready to talk about needs and wants?"

"Yes," we say in unison.

For the rest of our time with Dr. Judy, we deal with our list of wants and needs and what things are realistic and what things are not. We come to a compromise and then set up our next appointment with her in a month. The time until our next appointment is supposed to give us a month to try out all that we discussed and agreed to.

A part of the intensive was to have a hotel stay booked so that we would not go straight home after the intensive but to a space that would allow us to relax or keep working on what was needed. I am happy we listened because now we are headed to Lake Travis for some much-needed couple's time. Liza is right; she does not spend time alone. Neither do we spend enough time together, just the two of us. Both of those things need to change.

Chapter 7: Liza

We are driving to Lake Travis. I texted my mother and Olivier's mother to see how the kids were doing. We never send all of them to either parent. Our children can be a lot to handle. There is a comfortable silence surrounding us. I expected the intensive to help us but not as well as it did. Finally, having the conversation that we had been avoiding for years helped clear the air and allowed us to think about our future together. *I still really love my husband*, is the thought going through my mind as I look into the darkness of Texas as we drive. That thought makes me think about the day I fell in love with Olivier.

The Order was having its famous Mardis Gras Ball. It was for members and their spouses only. For the first time, Olivier was not singing at the event. The Order had hired J Crew Brass Band, the best in the city. I sat with Christy on one of the plush diamond-encrusted chaise lounge chairs that lined the ballroom's black accent wall. The ballroom was grand in that it held mirrored ceilings and a dozen beautifully handmade chandeliers. There was a faux cherry blossom tree in the corner that looked exceptionally real if it was not for the diamonds that accented the leaves. Christy and I had just sat down, and the band was setting up as the DJ's set had not yet ended. The DJ played different kinds of music that kept everyone engaged in the party no matter the member's age. As we sat, Christy told me about this guy named Trevor that she had just met and how he was a student at Tulane, and she couldn't wait to see him again. I was happy for her because Christy was rarely really interested in anyone. She was always too busy to notice people. Like, I was one to talk.

As Christy described Trevor, it seemed like heaven opened up and sent me an angel. He looked utterly enamoring. I know I said he was Finnnne before, but when he came into the room that night, Olivier looked like pure heaven. He had on a royal purple tailored suit that fit his muscular arms and legs to perfection. Even as he walked toward us, I could see the flexing of his thighs. He paired a black shirt with the Order's Mardi Gras-themed tie that all the brothers had to wear, and he had finished off his suit with a pair of purple Mardi Gras-themed oxfords. His locs had been freshly twisted and edged and placed into a neat design that pulled some back into an elaborate fishtail, and some were left to hang on his shoulders. His beard shined with a unique handmade sheen he bought from his loctician. He wore black diamond studs in his ears that spoke to the bad boy that laid just beneath the surface. I saw him lick his lips as he approached us. It was then that I finally made eye contact. His eyes spoke words that I was sure had left my thong saturated with the moisture that had accumulated there. His eyes held me captive as he made his final steps to the edge of my space.

"Hello, Belle. You look especially delectable tonight." I saw his eyes peruse my shoulders that lay bare in my off-the-shoulder black and purple bandaged dress that flared into little ruffles right above my knees. Then his eyes dropped to my legs which were sans stockings and ended with my freshly pedicured feet sandalled into the heels of my red bottoms. I saw him scan me once more and then arch an eyebrow at my shoes.

That is when, Christy reminded us of her presence when she said, "I know, right. Your girl did not by the knock-off this time." I elbowed her because I hated that term. "Oh, sorry, the faux version." She chuckled as she looked at me. I heard that dark chuckle leave from Olivier as well.

I stood, "Forget you both." I stated as I started to walk away.

"Oh, Liza, I didn't mean anything by it. He is the only other person that knows." Christy said.

"Belle, come back." I felt him grab my arm, and at that moment, the DJ started playing one of my favorite songs. "Sweet Lady" by Tyrese. It was an old song but my jam all the same.

"Belle, dance with me?" I turned and looked into those cognac-colored eyes that always seemed to intoxicate me.

"Ok," was my reply.

He walked us to the dance floor, wrapped my arms around his neck, and then put his hands on my hips. I looked up into his eyes, and I ran my fingers on the exposed skin at the nape of his neck. His gaze darkened at the feel of my fingers on his skin. He brought me in closer until I was thoroughly flushed against him. This was the closest that we had ever danced together. He moved his hand to the arch of my lower back, and we swayed to the sounds of Tyrese. We stared into each other's eyes as if no one else was there. Truthfully, they could have all left because I no longer saw them anyway. Then he started singing the song to me.

"Say you will be my baby, say you will be my lady, I've got to have all your love, so I won't even front, just say you'll give it to me, don't wanna hear the maybe's, and I will give you all my heart, if you say you'll be my baby...."

As he sang, he held my gaze like he meant every word. As the chorus came back around, I broke eye contact and laid my head on his chest. And Olivier continued to sing with Tyrese as he danced us around. The DJ put on another slow song, and we continued to dance. I eventually peered back up at Olivier, and when our eyes met, I saw the most sincere look of love and adoration that I have ever seen on him. He didn't say anything, just took one of my hands down, kissed the back, and then led me outside to the terrace. When we got there, he led us to a corner, and he pushed my back into the wall. He searched my eyes for permission.

I said, "Please, Olivier." And then he kissed me for the first time. His lips were tentative at first, cautious even. Then I put my arms around his neck, and he began to explore my lips, sucking my top lip into his mouth. When his tongue sought entrance, I opened my mouth and our tongues danced. I explored his depths and tasted him. He tasted of peppermint and strawberries and a unique favor I could only assume was him. Our kiss became more and more passionate until we almost consumed each other in the corner. His hand had pushed up the hem of my dress, so his palms were on my bare thighs, and he was pressed so close to me I could feel his erection as it built near my stomach. I moaned into him, and he groaned into me. It was the most explicit kiss I had ever shared, and to my surprise, I wanted more, so much more.

Then we heard someone clear their throat. I don't know how many times they had because my mind was clouded with Olivier. I couldn't even hear the cars below us. The person cleared their throat again, and we released each other's mouths. Olivier straightened my dress and then leaned his forehead into mine. He kissed my nose, making me smirk, then he looked into my eyes. If I was mistaken about the love and adoration I saw before, I was definitely not mistaken now. His eyes told me the things he wanted to say that he didn't and things he wanted to do that we couldn't out here. It was then that everything in me shifted for this man. I fell in love right there on the terrace.

When we released each other and Olivier turned around, keeping a hand on my thigh and standing in front of me, I heard his mother.

"Olivier, you know this is not the place for that. And Ms. Monroe," I leaned to the side so she could see me. "I expected more from you." With that, she turned to walk away.

I felt the hand that Olivier had on my thigh tighten.

"What is that supposed to mean, Mother?"

Lady LeBlanc turned around and walked up to her son. She sized him up. Their exchanges were always weird. "I meant I did not expect Ms. Monroe to be on the terrace involved in a make-out session, at an Order event, no less."

"Is that it? Are you sure you were not saying that in reference to me?"

"Dante, I do not think that little of you. Contrary to what you think, I love you. I just do not like the choices you have been making. This is not the time for this conversation, Dante."

"Then when?" His grip tightened again.

She sighed. "Fine, what?"

"What?" He released my thigh to use his hands to talk. "You act like I am less than the rest of this family because I have not chosen what I wanted to become or because I am choosing to sing."

"Oh, Dante, if you really wanted to be a singer and that was your dream, I would support you. If that were the career you really wanted, I would be at every gig. But the truth is, singing is not what you want for your life. Are you good at it? Yes, great even." She walked into his space and put her hand on his cheek. I saw him flinch, then relax and lean into her hand. "But Dante, Darling, it is not what you want. Singing is something you are doing to pass the time, but not to live. I just want you to find what makes you want to get up and go to work every day. The something that brings you joy and makes you proud to talk about."

She dropped her hand and then moved to the rail of the balcony and looked at the city below. Then she continued, "Maybe I have been going about this all wrong. You were always the one that responded to tough love. Maybe that is not what you need anymore." She turned to look at him, and for the first time in the two and half years that I had known them, she looked like a loving and caring mother. Not the mother that was disappointed and ready to disown him, but the mother that wanted what was best for him. I saw him walk to her.

He sighed and replied, "Mother, I just need some support. Tough love is not working with this. The more you push, the harder it is for me to figure it out." He paused and looked past her and then back. "I love you, and you are right. I am just passing the time by singing. But it is a part of whatever I am to do. I will figure it out, and then I will move forward and get another degree or whatever I need, but right now, can you just stop pushing so hard and love on me. I know what I need to do, ok?"

I saw the tears forming in her eyes, and then she brought him in for a hug. "Ok, Olivier. Ok."

I stood there and watched their moment with tears in my own eyes. The next thing I knew, Christy and Monsieur LeBlanc were coming outside, worried and then relieved once they saw Lady LeBlanc and Olivier hugging. The father and daughter joined the hug turning it into one big family hug. It was like finally, the broken family could heal. Finally, they could be loving and kind to each other. Monsieur LeBlanc turned to look at me, and I smiled. Then he opened one of his arms, inviting me into the family hug. It was an invitation I was glad to accept. From that moment on, things with Olivier and his family were better, and they welcomed me as one of them.

Chapter 8: Liza

Back to a year ago, after the intensive

"Belle, I will go check us in and get the key. Wait here. Ok?"

"Ok." With that, Olivier got out of the car. We had pulled up to a rather large resort facility. I could not see much of the resort, mainly just the outline, because it was dark outside. I could see that the building we had just driven up to was tall and wide. I watched him walk up to some very impressive wooden doors with anchors as door handles.

Olivier came out shortly after and drove us down a winding road closer to the lake. We had been to the lake before, but we had never stayed here. We pulled up to what looked like a bungalow that led into the lake. He got out of the car and opened my door.

"You can go ahead in. I will get the luggage." He hands me the key, and I go toward the entrance. The truth is we have not said much to each other since leaving the intensive. My husband is not much of a talker, so I try to go with it and just read the in-betweens. At least the air between us has been lighter than the tension we have been carrying for years.

When I open the red door, I am in total awe. There are candles lit all over the space. There are rose peddles that I follow through the living room space to the glass window that shows me roses in the lighted private pool that is in our backyard and the lake that is dimly lit by the moon behind us. I turn around and take in the living room space, with its light blue sofa and a glass coffee table arranged with red roses covering it. There is a TV mounted on the wall and a fireplace beneath it. When I turn to the other side, there is a kitchenette and on the bar is a bucket of wine with two wine glasses and some chocolate-covered goodies. I walk up to it to examine the goodies, and there is a note that says,

Couples need a Poweress Moment too!

Welcome to the first Power Couple's Retreat. The theme is Honesty. Together you can conquer the world, but you must be honest with yourselves and each other. The future awaits you. Let's Poweress Couples.

P.S. This is our first gift to you. There is more upstairs.

Love,

Your Poweress Committee.

Oh, My Gaud!! How did he do this? I didn't even know they were having one of these. Usually, I get emails about the Poweress' upcoming events, but I didn't see this. I read the letter once more and then turned to go upstairs.

I hear the front door open as I make it to the top. I walk into the bedroom area. There are red roses all over the floor and bed, and candles light the entire space. The room is like a loft, looking down to the living room below. The bed has a high back upholstered headboard with posts that extend from behind the headboard on either side, making it look like a bed intended for royalty. Beautiful shells outline the headboard, and sheer fabric runs across the bed's four posts. The opening that looks into the living room area also allows you to look through the windows that I didn't realize were floor-to-ceiling windows. I can see the moonlighting of the lake and the houses in the distance. When I turn, I see a set of double doors that fold open to reveal an impeccable white and gray master bathroom. When I walk into the bathroom, the first thing in front of me is a countertop made of shattered glass, and the double sinks are made of large iridescent seashells. There is a deep jacuzzi tub for two and a shower off to the left of the bathroom. Then to the right is a small closet, and the toilet is closed in its own separate space. Red roses are floating in a small amount of water in the sinks and the tub with sets of floating candles. When I come back out, I see the dresser in front of the bed with a TV mounted above it, and on the dresser is a box. The tag reads, *Open, Please.* I open the box to find three smaller boxes. They are labeled Arrival, Day 1, and Day 2. I open the box that says Arrival. There is everything from Yoni wash to Sensual (the yoni perfume) to Sexual (the personal lubricant) to a Rose Bud vibrator to a long feather that is so soft to handcuffs (cushioned, of course) to a Power Couples Devotional to matching amazonite mala necklaces to a pair of garnet ring bands set in beautiful white gold and diamonds. At the bottom of the box, there is a letter.

To say that we put a lot into your arrival gift is an understatement, but we believe that as couples, the Poweress and the Powerer need to know how to communicate on all levels, from sexual to spiritual. The devotional will assist you in going before God together so that you can be on one accord. The mala beads are in amazonite as it is a stone that will assist you in communicating openly and clearly in a safe and loving space. The garnet rings are set so that each of you can have one. It will stimulate intimacy and ignite the spark of passion and romance. We hope that tonight you will take a moment and have medivotion together, meditating and allowing God to speak to you together. Tomorrow breakfast will be delivered to your room at 8:30am, and then we will begin our session later that morning.

Enjoy your evening,

Your Poweress Committee

I smile at the letter. When I look up, Olivier is standing at the top of the stairs and leaning against the wall, looking as mesmerizing as the first time I saw him. *Oh, how I love this man*, I say to myself.

"So, Belle, what do you think? Surprised?" His voice holds more bass due to the late hour. It's the tone that he sings in when he is trying to set the mood for the audience.

"Very. I didn't even get notified about this."

"They only told the men on purpose. They said something like we, as the man, the Powerer, in the couple, should be the ones to go out and help our marriages walk in the honesty of purpose. You know how the committee tends to word things."

"Yeah......This place is gorgeous, and these gifts are perfect." I look up to see him staring at me with a smile in his eyes.

I walk over to him, and for the first time in way too long, I truly hug my husband as I say, "Thank you." He doesn't hug me back at first, but when I squeeze him close, I feel him sigh and squeeze me in. I smell that wonderful scent of wood, musk, and maple, and just like so many years ago, it is warm and inviting, charming and freeing all at once. I want to wrap myself in him and give him all I have to offer. We stand there hugging for a long while. Sometimes you don't realize how much you miss hugging until you have gone for so long without one. I hug and kiss my kids every day, but with them, it is different. Hugging Olivier fills my heart, my body, and my soul. It makes me feel loved and safe, like anything and everything is possible.

I feel him lift his head, and then I lean back and look at him. I see his eyes searching mine, asking me questions, and looking for my answers.

"Belle, I love you." He starts.

"Kiss me, Olivier."

With that, he leans in and kisses me deeply, allowing his lips to slide over mine feverishly. He seeks more of me, and I open my mouth, and he completely devours me, and a moan escapes me before I take my next breath. I give as much as I am given, and before long, he has picked me up and has me pinned against the wall as he makes love to my mouth. I groan deeply into his mouth. It has been too long since we have shared a moment like this. Since we have sought the same kind of intimacy and longing from one another. Just as we start to grind into each other, he stops and breathes. The need for oxygen comes before we can continue to feast on each other. He leans his forehead against mine and kisses my nose, just as he used to. I smile at the familiar tingle. He smiles and stands up straight. I arch an eyebrow at him in question. *Why is he stopping?*

"I don't want to rush this." That is what he says to my silent inquiry. I nod.

After a beat, he asks, "Bath with me?"

"Of course," I say, With that, he grabs the luggage I did not see at first and takes it into the bathroom closet. We undress slowly, watching the other as if we have never seen them before. My husband's body is toned, and his smooth pure, ebony skin is still as vibrant and erotic today as the first day I met him. Of course, with time, he is bigger in some places, but he has turned those places to a nice thickness that makes me feel even safer when I am in his presence and in his arms. When he removes his green boxer briefs, my breath hitches in my throat, his member has always been a place of awe to me, from its long length to its smooth head and veiny sides to its delicious dark chocolate color that melts in my mouth and not in my hand to the width of him that makes my mouth water. I lick my lips at the thought. I watch as he comes over with bath oils and body wash in hand and puts them on the lip of the tub. I turn to the tub and start the water, placing the oils and herbs that the committee left into the water. They really think of everything. Then I finish removing my dress. I am not facing him, but I hear his breathing change as I stand before him in my matching bra and panty set. It is funny because before meeting Christy, matching sets were not my thing. One of the most beautiful lessons from the Order was that, as a woman, I have to learn to indulge myself in things that make me feel good. If my man happens to like it, that is just a plus. I have tried many a combination and many a brand, but the one I love the most and the one that gets Olivier breathing as deeply as he is now is Agent Provocateur. It is the brand that makes me feel the most luxuriously provocative.

I turn around and watch as his gaze scans my body. It amazes me the kind of adoration he still holds in his gaze as he looks at my body. Whereas his body is pretty much the same, mine no longer is small and lean and blemish-free. Now, I am rounder in places that were once flat, thicker in areas that were once lean, fuller in places that were once small, and have stretch marks that are the tiger stripes from the journey of bringing life into the world. The once size 4 woman he married is now a full size 16, on a good day. However, you would not know the difference in the way that he is looking at me and licking his lips. He stares as if I am his prey. It turns me on. I must admit.

However, my slight insecurity in this new skin causes me to turn around and remove the rest of my clothes. As I go to unlatch my bra, I feel him behind me. He grabs the latch and shoos away my hands. He turns off the water running in the tub. Then, before he unhooks my bra, he whispers in my ear.

"Belle, you are the most beautiful woman I have ever known. Can I help you see what I see?"

I nod. He runs his hands down my thighs and across my hips as he whispers, "You have curves that make me want to...". He licks the rim of my ear. Then he takes his hands, squeezes my ass, and makes me arch my back into him. "An ass that makes me want to...." He bends me over and allows me to feel the fullness of his erection that was not there before. Then he stands me up slowly and runs a hand up my back, and slight shiver releases from me. He slowly unlatches my bra, and my full 36 DDs fall free. He catches them in his hand, squeezes gently, and says, "A pair of the most luscious breast that makes me want to......" He kisses down my shoulder and then the side of my breast. A moan escapes me. He comes around in front of me, looking at my lips. He stares for a moment and then says, "And lips that haunt my dreams with their softness on both my mouth and my dick. It makes me want to......" He engulfs my lips in the most feverish kiss I have ever had. Then he looks me in the eyes as he splays his hands across my stomach. I cringe. He shakes his head no, and then he lays his hand across my stomach again. I don't cringe this time, and he smiles. He encircles my waist with his arms, and while looking into my eyes, he says, "You have the abdomen that brought the most precious gifts I have ever received into this world. The place where life from my seed grew and was nourished by you until its birth. All of you makes me want to...." He keeps his eyes on me as he kisses down my mouth to my neck, down the valley between my breast, across my stomach, and he dips his tongue ever so slightly into my belly button and swipes around it in small circles before he travels south and inhales the essence of my femininity. I am wetter than wet. My desire can be smelled all around me of that, I am sure. He looks up at me with darkened eyes, and he slowly removes my underwear. "You have the most amazing pussy I have ever had the pleasure to enjoy then, and now, it makes me want to......" He grabs my leg and puts it on his shoulder as he dips his head and kisses my lower lips as if they were my upper pair. He takes his tongue and makes deliciously slow and then fasts circles around my clit, and then he hums the tune that became our song. I moan and rock into him. He begins to feast on me, like I am his favorite meal, and he cannot get enough. Before long, my legs are too weak to hold me, and I begin to shake. He then lays on the floor, pulls me down to his face, and says, "Belle, will you ride my face and moisturize my beard?"

I let out a laugh, but oh, how I do oblige. It has been too long since I have allowed him to taste me, let alone ride his face. I ride like my life depends on it, and when I look down, his eyes are on me. It makes me moan, and I hear him groan beneath me. I grab his hardened member, and I pump him slowly. Dragging out the precum, I feel starting to wet my palm. He is so hard, and I want so much more. I turn around, keeping my core planted on his lips. I position his dick at the entrance of my mouth and begin to taste the taste that is all Olivier. It is my favorite dessert. I hear him groan, and his hips start to pump as I pick up the pace, twirl my tongue around him, and use my hand to pump. Then I feel him put two fingers inside of me, and I scream. "Oh, my Gaud!!!" I go back to sucking, and then I lean forward, causing him to release me as I suck his balls into my mouth.

"Shit, Belle!!"

I go back to sucking his length, and he repositions me over his mouth. I am riding and almost on the verge of what I know will be orgasmic ecstasy. As the pressure rises within me, I know he knows my orgasm is coming. It is like he always knows because he begins to suck and flick faster, and then he sticks a finger into my ass, and I come undone screaming his name over and over again. This time is no different, in the most delicious of ways. As I fall apart, I feel him lay me on the beautiful white and gray plush rug beneath us. Then he positions himself over me. He looks into my eyes, seeking permission for something he should never have to ask me for, but here we are. On the moan that still courses through me, I moan, "Yes, please Olivier. Please." With that, he plunges into me in one full stroke. It feels like the most erotic homecoming I have ever had. He is still for a moment, and when I look into his eyes, I can see the same feelings of home, hope, longing, and missing that is playing through me. He begins to rock in and out of me slowly as if he is savoring the moment and every stroke. I rock into him, and our hips move in sync, bringing us closer and closer to the release we seek, all while joining us. I take a deep breath and use my vaginal muscles to bring him even deeper into me. Allowing my soul to open up to this man who I was once one with but have shied away from. As I let my spirit and heart open up and receive him, I gaze into his eyes, and I see the moment he receives what I am offering and the moment he begins to open himself to me. I feel the spiritual connection between us, and we move as one. The tears start to fall from my eyes as the union we share is reestablished just as my second orgasm takes hold of me, and I scream his name until I have no more sound to give. My eyes roll back into my head, and I shatter into pieces. I feel him speeding up his strokes as his orgasm rises, and when I open my eyes, I see the tears that have formed within his. I see the connection we have and the destiny we want, and then I squeeze my yoni, and he releases into me, whispering my name in orgasmic emptying. He lays on me, making me feel safe and protected in our love.

When the aftershocks of our lovemaking have ceased, he leans upon his forearms, with his dick still inside me.

"Liza, Belle, I love you."

"Olivier, I love you too." I wrap my arms around my husband, and he removes himself from me. He picks me up, and we slide into the tub, add in a little hot water, and start the jets. I lean against his front with my back, and he moves my head to rest in the crook of his neck, and we breathe together. With our hearts, our souls, and our breathing synced as one.

Chapter 9: Olivier

We talked after our bath, and she allowed me to lead us into medivotion together. We prayed for our present and future, for God to provide all the increase, strength, and wisdom we needed. We cleared and anointed our mala necklaces and the rings from the committee and used the mala necklaces for the meditation portion of medivotion. We stared into each other eyes and breathed deeply together, and then we allowed ourselves to feel God's presence together. We sat in the peace of God for I don't know how long. Then I heard him say, "It will be well. You guys will be fine. Love her, respect him."

When I opened my eyes, she was staring at me. She asked if I had just heard what God said. It was crazy. For the first time, we literally heard him simultaneously, in the same breath. After our medivotion was over, we put on the garnet rings, and then I kissed her. I have missed this openness to touch each other for so long. So much so, that I could not seem to keep my hands to myself, and the responses she gave said she did not want me to. So, we made love again on the carpet and eventually in the bed.

I awoke to the knock on the door with breakfast. I went to get it, came back, and laid back in bed. Now, I am sitting here and watching Liza sleep. Last night was the most beautiful experience. We indeed became one. I felt her, and she felt me, and it was mind-blowing. Then to hear God together. I am beyond grateful. When I signed us up for this retreat, I was unsure if it would be a good idea. After all, we were in an all-day intensive yesterday, and I had no idea how that would end. But when I got the email, I heard God say, "Do it." So, I did, and now I am glad I was obedient. We made lots of strides yesterday and last night, but I know we will definitely need strength to continue to walk in this space.

"Thank you, God," I say aloud and kiss Liza on the forehead.

She begins to stir. Then she opens those beautiful green hazel eyes and stretches. She looks toward me, and I smile. *God, I love this woman*, I say to myself.

"Were you watching me sleep?"

"Yes." She smiles and sits up, and straddles me. It seems like I am not the only one who can't keep my hands to myself. She kisses my neck near my ear and whispers, "Good Morning, Olivier."

I wrap my arms around her, "Good morning, Belle." Then we sit and share a morning hug. It is peaceful and rejuvenating to my soul. I rub my hands up and down her back, "Breakfast is here. We have about an hour before we need to be at the session."

"Ok." She stretches again and wiggles her hips.

"We don't have time for that."

"You can't make time, Mr. LeBlanc?" I growl at her. She laughs as I flip her over, enter her smoothly, and have a morning round of newfound blissed oneness before eating breakfast and getting dressed.

****

Liza comes out of the bathroom as I am putting on my shoes. I look at her and smile. She is wearing a pair of pants that fit her thighs like a second skin until it flares out at the knee into a bell bottom. The pants are black. When she turns to the side, I see that the pants tie up at the sides, making me think if I just pulled the strings, her pants would fall, giving me easy access. I smirk and stand to my feet. She has on the high low gray sweater that I bought her this Christmas. It is loose-fitting but drops down in the front giving a nice view of her cleavage if she wants to show it. Today, she must want to, as I can see her gorgeous breast waving at me as she puts her hair into a ponytail. The sweater covers that sweet ass but exposes her midriff when she lifts her hands.

She is doing all this stalling for my benefit, I am sure. I learned a long time ago that my wife becomes very nonverbal when it comes to sex. I see the smile playing on her freshly glossed lips as she walks out of the bathroom. She is wearing minimal make-up, and I love the freshness of her natural beauty. It was one of the things I noticed about her first. She needs no assistance. I smile as I see the flirt playing in her eyes, and then I look to see what her hands are doing. She is not doing what I thought at all. She is putting something in her hair that allows her natural curl to shine through, which makes me moan. I love a woman with her natural curls. From the softness of the curls to the fact that I can pull them and she won't be mad, but mainly the fact that the woman wearing them is free enough in herself that she lets the pure beauty of her crown loose, that is genuinely a turn-on for me. Liza used to wear her curls, but once the business she helped create went public, she took on a corporate appearance. She was gorgeous in her corporate attire, but that was not the Liza I knew. I accepted it all the same because I understood it. How could I not? I knew that if I ever went into corporate America, they would make me cut my waist-length locs. Therefore, I am not in corporate America. My locs are a representation of my life and journey with God. So cutting them is a decision that He and I make alone.

With these thoughts in mind, I look back into her eyes and see her smiling. As I walk up to her, I finally speak, "Belle, did I mess up your hair last night?" I smirk.

She chuckles, "Yes, that bath was eventful." I laugh.

She turns around, going back into the bathroom to ensure she has finished what she was doing. I look at her through the mirror as she fluffs her hair. She stares at me, then she places a hand on her hip and asks, "How do I look?"

"Delectable." I lick my lips. She shakes her head and chuckles. She gets her shoes from the closet and takes them to the bed.

"I decided it was time to be me. It has been a long time since I let my hair be in its natural state. Always flat ironing it takes a lot of work." I lean against the door as she talks. I say nothing. Silence passes between us.

"I heard you last night about what you see." She pauses and peers up at me. "I see it. My hair is a nice reflection of that."

I smile at her and then look at the box with the gifts in it. We have about 15 minutes before we need to leave at this point. I open the big black box and find a small purple box labeled Day 1. I take it out and open it. I admire the inside lining of black velvet and then take out the two smaller boxes within. They say His and Hers. I turn and hand Liza the Hers just as she pulls her Valentino crossbody over her head. She takes her box and begins to open it. I turn to mine and open it. Within it is something unexpected. It is a silver money clip with a diamond accent at the end. The engraving reads:

I am Honest with Me, and also with You.

Folded into the money clip is a note,

Never forget that marriage requires you to work on yourself as well as you guys. Your spouse is there to assist you and respect you. She will love and support you if you let her.

Poweress Committee.

I read the note again. I know this is true, but I also know that in an attempt to lead, I do not always allow Liza to be there for me, not the way I need at times. I take the cash out of my pocket and remove my old clip. One that I got a long time ago. I put on the new money clip and placed my old one with my other items on the dresser. It is then that I hear the sniffle coming from Liza. I turn around, and sure enough, I see her sitting on the bed and wiping a stray tear. In her hand is something that looks like lipstick with a diamond at the end and engraving. I kneel beside her and put my hand on her leg.

"Belle?" She smiles down at me and hands the lipstick to me. I read the engraving:

I am Honest with Me, and also with You.

Then she hands me the note that I guess came with it:

Let your lips speak the honesty that lives within your heart. There is no reason for worry, for your husband can handle it. He loves you.

Poweress Committee.

"It's a lipstick case." She takes out one of her Pat McGrath Lipsticks. I only know because I see the bill. She places the lipstick in the case, and it is a perfect fit. I sit next to her and show her the money clip and note. She smiles at me.

"We can do this, Belle. I am here for this." I say as I put my hand on her heart.

"So am I." She leans in, places her hand on my heart, and then kisses me softly.

After a moment, we get our things together and head to the session.

****

The morning session started with group medivotion. Carmello and Christine are the practitioners. They put us in groups with two other couples, so each group has six people, and then we all share space in medivotion and have a small conversation. During the session, they have a joint workshop about the meaning of honesty and why men and women have a hard time being honest. They were right, you want to tell your spouse things, but sometimes you are afraid of the outcome. Are you saying it right? Should you use another tone? Was the word choice insensitive? What will she think about what I am saying? Will me talking about my feelings turn into an argument? Why can't this whole thing be easy? Are women really born this way?

These are all the questions that go through my mind when I decide to share the honesty within me. It's not that I lie to Liza. I don't. I just don't always let her see my inner struggle. I was taught to be a man and handle emotions within. Shoot, really, I was taught I had no feelings, but that is not true. I definitely have feelings and emotions. Anyway, Liza listens when I tell her things. However, she sometimes has these analytical questions that I cannot answer, which leads me to frustration and anger. I know she knows I have feelings. Her parents raised her to appreciate both sides of an argument. After all, they are scientists. They just did not show her how to leave science at work and not let it take over her life. They are, just as my parents are, workaholics. The difference is Liza's parents left her with nannies to tend to her needs as they ran off to save the world with pharmaceuticals, and my parents took Christy and me with them as they worked in the Order tirelessly. We did have nannies, just not all the time. I don't want Liza and me to repeat the cycle on either side. I don't want nannies, and I don't want my kids to be drug to different events that have nothing to do with them all the time. I guess this means I need to start letting Liza know what I need. But how do I do that effectively?

I zone back into the workshop just as they say they are splitting up the sexes to have Powerer and Poweress conversations over lunch. We will then reconvene with our spouses for our couple's session. They say a text is going out with each couple's time and location. I stand, and Liza and I walk to the door. I kiss her nose, and we go our separate ways. As I walk to the Hour Room for lunch, I get the text:

LeBlanc's, your time is 3:30p in the Honey Suite on Level 4.

I nod. Then head to my session. The Hour Room is set up in a large conference room style with leather chairs and gourmet dinner plates sitting covered on the table. I walk into the room and find my name. I shake the hand of the man to my left, and then when I turn to my right, I am pleased to see a familiar face.

"Hakim, my dude! Long time no see, Brother." I dab him up as he stands to hug me. Hakim and I grew up together in New Orleans. We met during middle school, and his father was a member of the Order. We used to keep in touch, but things just fell off after we started having kids.

"Hey, Brother!"

We sit.

"So, where are you living now?" I ask him.

"Oh, we live in the Dallas area now. My wife has family out that way. What about you?"

"Houston," I say with an arched brow. He laughs. We used to joke that we would never live in Texas because it was too close to home, but here we are. We both used to say we wanted to live in another country altogether to get rid of the requirements of being sons to some of the highest-ranking men in the Order. But again, here we are.

"So, how are the valley and the mountain?"

"The valley still has harvest and the mountain still provides shade. Where are your graces?"

"High but never gone. Fresh mercy and grace every day, sustain the strong and the weary." With that, we shake hands in a way only a fellow brother of the Order would. We basically just told each other we are still active members in the Order, and we both have taken our rightful places, even though we have not been to the major joining where all chapters meet.

With that, we sit down and bring the fellas around us into a conversation, and we make small talk and eat lunch. Until Carmello walks into the room with leather-bound journals and gives one to each of us. The journal is beautifully made. It has intricate tribal designs pressed into its leather, and my name is pressed into it at the bottom with Power Couple in a smaller font beneath my name. We are then handed Mont Blanc pens that also say Power Couple. Our remaining dishes are collected, and Carmello sits at the head of the table. Carmello is the normal officiant and host during our Man of Power, Powerer Retreats, so we all know him and are familiar.

"Gentlemen, welcome. You know, when we decided to do this, I wanted to ensure that the fellas and the ladies would get something out of it. Not just tokens to think about but, in true Poweress fashion, something to live out. I want to start our sessions with you guys writing candidly to yourselves in your journals. Write the things you need to say to your spouse but have not. The things you need to admit to yourself but haven't. The things that need to be changed within you, but you have been too stubborn. Write what you want from her and why you haven't asked. And when you are done, we will begin. Please start."

I look at Hakim, and he arches a brow. Yeah, this is about to get real deep. I take a deep breath and think about all the things Carmello said and all the things Liza and I shared yesterday. I sit back and let my mind genuinely think about what I needed to say to her and to myself. Then it hits me full fledge. I pick up the pen and begin to write:

My feelings do not always show how I truly feel them. I worry more about how you are than how I am. I have spent so much time waiting to reunite with you that now that I have you again, how do I keep you? How do I ensure that we do not go back down that road? How do I make sure that you know yourself and see yourself? How do I ensure that you are provided for, and our kids are provided for? How do I keep you all happy? How do I make sure that we are all happy? How do I do this?

Then I hear that voice that is always soft and gentle with me. The voice that sets me straight and loves on me. The voice of the only one I ever allow to see me broken and vulnerable. I hear God say, "Son, stop worrying. You don't have to do all those things; I do. Let me lead through you.

Let me lead you so that you can lead them. Regularly, come before me together, as husband and wife, and your marriage will be great. Give yourself and her space to come to me separately, and then you will both see yourself as I see you and see each other as I see you. Then you can love better and parent better. Stop putting this on your shoulders. It is mine to carry. Let me lead, and you follow me, Olivier."

As He spoke, I wrote, and when He stopped, I took a deep breath and let it all marinate into my being. God is right, of course. All of the things I am worried about are for Him to fix. I just need to be the head He called me to be, and to do that, I need to follow Him. I pick up my pen and begin to write again:

I will follow the Lord and allow Him to lead me so that I can lead us. It is not how do I but did He.

What I want is the unity and oneness we had last night all the time. I want the way I feel today forever. I know that things will not always be good, but I want to know that we are always on the same side and that you will always have my back because I will always have yours. I want to know that I am not in this alone but that you are here with me for the long haul. I want you, Liza.

Then God speaks again, "And she wants you. You want the same thing. Trust me."

I write what He says, and I truly believe Him. Just as I am taking a moment to breathe, Carmello calls time.

"I want you to think about what you just wrote. Do you think you could share that with your wife?" He pauses, then says, "What do you think, to share with your wife or not share, and why?" He is asking the guy on my left. This share or not share conversation goes around, and as it does, I wonder should I share this with Liza. My spirit says yes that I can trust her. So I decided that if the opportunity presented itself, I would share my thoughts with her.

As I tune back into the conversation, I hear Carmello saying, "Gentleman, I know that we have been told to keep our feelings and emotions close to the heart. Not to show them and not to share them. The problem is in a marriage that does not work. Because as much as we want her to learn to respect us, she needs us to love her, and loving her looks like being transparent with her. She wants to know that just as she has divulged her heart to you that you will do the same for her." At that moment, the door opens, and Christine, the other host, comes in.

"Am I too early?" She smiles sweetly at Carmello and then nods to all of us.

"No, Dear, you are right on time. I just told them ladies want us to share our hearts with them." He pauses as she reaches his side, and he kisses her forehead. "Gentlemen, I know you have met Christine, but what you do not know is she is my wife of 30 years." Every man in the room lets out a long breath. Carmello and Christine chuckled at our antics.

"Powerers, it is my pleasure to meet you. Do you mind if I say a couple of things as Mello goes to speak with the ladies?" She looks each man in the eye and waits on his answer individually. When we have all agreed, Carmello kisses her forehead again and takes his leave.

"I know what Carmello said is hard to do. You don't know what her response will be. You don't know if she will look at you differently if you let her know the truth and let her see that you don't have it all together." We all agree with her. "The truth is she will love you all the more because of your openness. She will see it as a strength and respect and protect it, just as you do for her. Real women are not afraid of your emotions because they understand the risk you took to share them. They understand that at that moment, they can be a better helpmate than they have ever been because now they have your whole picture, the logic you are so gifted to share, and the emotions you are not sure what to do with. Truthfully, God has made it so that you have the logic and physical strength on lock, and she has the emotions and details. Together you can conquer anything that comes your way. If only you let the other person help you in the areas you need. She can carry your emotions because she knows how to read and hold them, just as you can add the line of logic to her rambling of details. After all, you were born to see the logic. We all represent one side of the coin, and our spouse is the other side of the same coin, or you could say she is the yin to your yang. Together you are balanced and ready for destiny. Any thoughts?" She looks at us intently.

One of the fellas raises his hand, she acknowledges him, and he says, "What if she closed you down before? What if you were honest about your feelings and she shut you down? Men do not keep reinitiating that kind of thing." We make our grunts of agreement.

She nods and then speaks, "I am sorry to any of you who have gone through that. I know it is not easy to be closed down by the person you love. I will say this sometimes when she does not have her own emotions intact, she cannot manage another's. Women do a poor job of managing another's feeling when she is not balanced herself. This is not an excuse for her closing you down. This, however, is the truth. As hard as it is, I will say you need to forgive her and then be honest with her about that moment when she closed you down and what that did to you. Allow her the opportunity to apologize, and if she is willing, give her another opportunity to show you she can and that she does care about your feelings and wants to be your helpmate. In marriage, we all make mistakes, but we have to choose to work through the issues, forgive each other, make a plan to move forward, and then move forward. It is the only way for your marriage to continue growing and thriving."

"Thank you for that. I can receive that." The guy says, and some of us nod in agreement, me being one of them. This conversation confirms I should share with Liza and allow her to be there for me. I think that is the reason I started resenting her. I didn't feel like she was there for me. She was always just mad because of my duties in the Order, but honestly, how could she think another way if I had not even told her why I was obligated to the Order. As I allow these thoughts to circle within me, I realize I lied yesterday. Because I told her I did not resent her anymore, and I thought I didn't, but it wasn't until this moment that all of the resentment went away. It was not until I realized that she did not leave me to fend for myself; that I did that by myself, just as she had done with the clinic. At least with the clinic, she had not made a choice without me. However, I made a choice and took the issues that came with that choice out on her. I need to resolve this.

Carmello comes back in, and we do an Open Convo, which allows any man to ask any question about marriage, whether it is about the topic of honesty or not. The conversation was great. We talked about work, needing me time as the ladies called it, sex and making love, and all kinds of other things. When we were dismissed, it was about 3:25p.

So, now I am headed to the Honey Suite. Before I go, Hakim and I dab up one more time and promise to get in touch in the coming weeks. We both still have the same number. With that, I am on my way.

****

When I get to the room, Liza is sitting on the chaise, scrolling through her phone. Knowing her, it is probably Pinterest. She hears the door close behind me, and she looks up and gives me a smile. I sit next to her and wrap an arm around her back, letting my hand sit next to her hip.

"How was your session, Belle?"

"Good. Yours?"

"Insightful." She is still scrolling through Pinterest, as I said. I put my hand on her arm, and she looks up at me.

"Is everything ok?"

"I need to say something, as it is on my mind."

With that, she turns into me, but before I start talking, our practitioners come in. "I apologize. Can you give us a minute?" I ask them.

"Sure. Just knock on this side door when you are ready." With that, the practitioners go back out. When I look back at Liza, the concern is etched on her beautiful face.

"Olivier, what is it?" She asks with her hand on my jean-clad thigh.

"I realized I lied to you yesterday, and I wanted to apologize." I then go into what happened during our session and how I realized this, and I conclude with, "I am sorry for lying, and I can honestly now say I do not resent you at all."

She is staring at me with this weird shocked but pleased look on her face. I know I said a lot, but the face she is giving me is starting to worry me. After a moment, she speaks, "I think that is the most descriptive you have ever told me a story." She pauses. I stare at her, perplexed. *Was that a compliment?* I think to myself.

"I'm sorry. I am in shock, I think." She takes a deep breath and fiddles with her phone, and when she looks back up, her eyes are filled with joy. "Thank you for sharing with me, Olivier, and I completely understand. I am happy we are on the same page now and that you don't resent me. Is there a way that we could give some of the money back to the Order? We could use my paycheck, or can we split some of your duties where I do some of the things. That way, you have some time to yourself that is not about the Order."

I don't know what to say to what she just stated. I would never have thought to ask her those things, but as I am thinking about it, they are actually really good ideas. I pull her into my lap so that she is straddling me.

"Olivier, they are waiting on us. We can't do that in here." She whispers.

I kiss her gently, and when she opens her mouth, I consume her. I breathe in her exhale and explore her mouth. She tastes of Liza and chocolate, and just when she moans into my mouth, I suck on her bottom lip and release her mouth. I give her one more peck.

"First off, Yes, we can do that, anywhere" I grab her ass and grind her into me until she moans, "because you are mine. Second off," I lift her chin so that her eyes are on me, "thank you for your offers. I would not have ever thought to ask you for any of that. Let me look into some things and think about it, and I will let...Actually, I will look into it and think about it, and then you and I can have a conversation on what is best after I get all the details. Deal?"

She smiles at me. My change in verbiage says we are learning.

"Deal," she replies. I kiss her nose and then her lips quickly. I sit her back on the chaise and go and knock on the door for the practitioners to come back in.

Chapter 10: Liza

We just finished Couples Reiki, where they helped align us together and as individuals. When the practitioners were done performing Reiki, they told us what God had told them, which was as long as we keep making an effort to be united, we would never be apart. We just had to make oneness and we-ness a priority. What they said confirmed how we felt over the last two days. Then they said they wanted to take a moment and give us our individual Reiki Revelations from God. So, we went to separate ends of the room.

Now I am walking up to the female practitioner; her name is Lauren. She pulls some items out of her bag and lays them on the seat. The bag is a beautifully embroidered purple bag that says Poweress Committee. It makes me wonder if the committee members get as wonderful of gifts as we do. I walk up to her, and she then turns around, holding a gold woven waist bead with clear quartz, moonstone, and garnet on it. The design of the waist bead is so detailed and intricate. She places two charms, a heart charm, and a Poweress charm, on the waist bead. Then she looks at me and holds the waist bead up.

"Do you mind if I tie you a waist bead as I talk?"

"No, not at all." I turn to face the mirror in the corner of the room. As I turn, I can see Olivier and the man talking out of the corner of my eye. I cannot hear them, though.

Lauren begins talking in that soothing voice she has been using since we started Reiki. It is calm and peaceful, just like the vibe in the room. "Liza, stop searching for you when she is already inside of you. You have done a great job of being honest about looking for you, but God is saying just be true to you. The Holy Spirit guides you day by day. He said your discernment and intuition tell you every moment who you are, what you want, and the choices you really want to make. But every day, you choose what you think is expected instead of who you are. When you actually start walking honestly in who you are, you will shine brighter than ever before. See, honesty persuades you to accept what is true, what is real, what is fact, and what is accurate. When you are honest with yourself, you accept what is true, what is real, what is fact, and what is accurate about and within you.

You are a beautiful woman inside and out. You know the truth, but it is time that you live honestly and live happily because truth sets us free. When we are honest with ourselves, we accept the truth about ourselves. Not someone else's truth about us, but the truth that comes from God through His revelation about who we are and who He has made us to be. Do you choose to be honest with yourself, accept yourself, and be truthful with others?"

At this point, I am crying because everything she said was true. During Reiki, I heard God say, "Liza, you already know who you are. I have shown you, and I show you every day. Stop being worried that other people cannot handle your truth. You just need to handle your honesty. I got you, and those who love you will fall in place."

Now, I stand here, and Lauren is asking me the question I was asking myself. Will I be honest with myself, accept the truth, and walk in it, or will I keep allowing fear of acceptance to hinder me? I am tired of not being who I am. I am tired of not being honest with myself about those things I love about myself that some other people may not. I want to be free, and just like in my marriage, to do that, I need to be honest with myself and truthful with others.

I must have been thinking for a while because I hear Lauren ask me again, "Do you choose to be honest with yourself, accept yourself, and be truthful with others?"

I take a deep breath and look into Lauren's patient eyes and say, "Yes, I choose to be honest with myself, accept myself, and be truthful with others from this day forward."

I wipe the tears away and take a deep breath. She smiles at me and says, "Great." With that, she ties my new waist bead, cuts away the excess beads, and steps back. I stand in the mirror looking at my waist bead, touching it, and realizing it feels so right on my body and on my fingers. As I stand there, allowing the new bead to become a part of me, I feel pure joy and freedom of living in my honesty. I look at Lauren in the mirror.

"Liza, I am so proud of you. I tied you with clear quartz for clarity across the board, but specifically clarity about you. The moonstone is for femininity and will help you walk in the feminine place that is your true self and the power that that brings. Moonstone is also to help you find those wonderful treasures that lay deep within you. The garnet is for grounding in God in every moment. Garnet, together with the moonstone, is to help you tap into your sensuality not just as a sexual force but also as a freeing and creative power. The garnet will also keep the passion between you and your husband flowing, which is why you were given the rings you share. Any questions?"

I shake my head no.

"I chose to tie you instead of using one of our clasp beads because I don't want you to go back to not living in honesty and truth. Tying you makes this new journey one that is intended to stick and one that you need to embrace fully. Now. Today." She turns around a picks up a gold and silver waist bead with clear quartz crystals, but this waist bead is exceptionally long. It also has a heart and a Poweress charm. It is magnificent. She places it over my head, and one-piece stays around my neck and drops between my breast while the other piece wraps around the top of my hips. I feel sexy and wanton. I look at her, ready for her to explain.

"This is a body chain. It is intended to make you feel sexy and also add a little extra assistance and push when you need it. It is clear quartz and hematite. Like the gold on your waist bead I tied, the gold represents royalty, and the silver represents wealth and strength. The clear quartz again is for clarity and also cleansing. The charms on both the body chain and the waist bead are the heart charm to remind you to love yourself, your husband, and God, and the Poweress charm reminds you that you are Poweress. When you walk true to your authentic self, you are far more powerful than you could ever dream. Honestly, walking in authenticity requires you to let God guide you to yourself, and it requires you to accept His guidance in order to accept yourself and be honestly and truly you."

I smile at her. It is all perfect. I turn and give her a big hug, and she hugs me back.

"Thank you so much, Lauren. This has truly blessed me beyond measure."

"You're truly welcome," she states with a slight nod. She hands me a bag to put the body chain in when I am not wearing it, and then she also gives me a black leather moto jacket with Power Couple embroidered on the front right shoulder, and then Poweress embroidered on the front left shoulder. Both sets of words are signed in white thread in the standard Poweress font I have come to love. Poweress has its signature butterflies on the last 'S.' On the back of the jacket is an amazingly detailed and embroidered cherry blossom tree that has hints of purple mixed in with its pink petals, and on the top, in the same font as Poweress is the word *Honesty* and on the bottom in the same font it says *Brings New Beginnings.* I pull the jacket to me. I love it. I give her another hug, and we say our goodbyes.

I turn as the male practitioner, Isaiah, gives Olivier his moto jacket. It looks the same as mine, except his left shoulder says Powerer in block letters with a phoenix on the last 'R,' and the words on the back are the same as mine but in that same block lettering as Powerer. Isaiah and Olivier give each other one of those manly hugs, where they clasp hands and come in. Then, Isaiah turns to me and nods his head, and I do the same. With that, Isaiah goes out of the same door that Lauren did. I bring my gaze back over to Olivier, and he smiles sweetly at me. It is a smile that I have not seen since our wedding. It is innocent and siren. It is perfect. I walk over to him, and he meets me halfway at the fireplace. He opens his arms, and we hug.

"Thank you for doing this," I say into the crook of his neck.

"My pleasure." He responds in that deep voice of his.

I lean back and say, "I love you, Olivier."

"I love you too, Belle."

He lifts my chin to him, and he kisses me gently.

Chapter 11: Olivier

Today has been a good day, from the Medivotion this morning to the sessions together and separately to the Couples Reiki. It has been excellent but tiresome too. I genuinely enjoy the Powerer Retreats. They always seem to relax me but challenge me at the same time. As I sit in our private pool and look at the moonlight, I think about what my practitioner said to me after Reiki.

"Olivier, transparency with your spouse, will not work if you are not honest with yourself. There is something that you have hidden deep inside of you. Something that sent you running for a long time. That thing is very much a part of who you are, and until you own that, you will not be free. You have to accept the truth of who you are and stop hiding. You need to be honest with yourself and your spouse."

When he said that, I had to stop myself from tearing up. The truth is, he was confirming what I heard God say while I was laying on the table during Reiki. But how? That is the question I am pondering as I sit in this heated pool and have a drink of Henny. How am I supposed to be honest with myself about something I was told to hide when I was a child. How am I supposed to live in the truth when the very person who told me to hide it is still such a big part of my life? How?

"Trust Me. The truth will set you free. Start with Liza." I hear God say. I take a deep breath and throwback my drink. That is easier said than done.

I hear Liza approaching by the soft step of her feet against the rocks. She has always had this smooth walk. It is like she wants to caress you with her steps before she gets to you. As she comes around into view, I cock my head to the side. She is wearing a hotel robe. She eyes me like she is reading my soul. I can tell she sees the intensity of my thoughts because the smile she originally wore is replaced with a firm lip. She gazes at me, waiting for me to stop the silence and share what is on my mind.

That is one thing I have always loved about Liza, she doesn't rush me to talk or process. She waits for me. Everyone else, my mom and dad and Christy, have always wanted me to talk more, to share my feelings more. They never try to wait. When I was about 7 years old, I started keeping my thoughts to myself. I stopped being so quick to share my feelings and hurts. I stopped trying to get those I love to hear my opinions. I realized then that my opinion didn't matter. I was to do what I was told. When I got older, in high school, everyone started wanting me to talk about my goals and what I wanted to do with my life. My sister, Christy, was and is the talker. She talks about it all. She was the only one I would share bits and pieces with, but again I never wanted to share. I always assumed they loved me, but they wouldn't like what I wanted, and sure enough, after college, when I started making music, shit hit the fan. I was supposed to be a pharmacist, which was the goal they set. But that was never my dream.

Anyway, I am sitting here holding my empty class and looking at my gorgeous wife as she analyzes my body language. Oh yeah, that is where I was going. See, when I met Liza, it was like seeing a dream, meeting my destiny, and falling in love on sight. Everything in me wanted to open up to her, get to know her, and let her know me. It was the reason I couldn't stay away even with the Order's rules. As time went on, I wanted to share more and more because she never judged me. She never looked at me like my goals weren't worthy of some unspoken rule. She just shared in the highs I had and in the lows. She would always encourage me to go for what I wanted, even when I told her my real dream of customizing instruments. She just smiled and told me she couldn't wait to see all the beautiful things she knew I would create.

I look at her now, as it seems she has decided what to do with my current state. She walks around the pool to my side and takes the glass out of my hand. She goes inside and returns with the bottle of Henny and my glass already filled with a double. She hands it to me and smiles. Then she pulls a second glass out of the robe pocket and pours another double. I arch a brow at her. Brown liqueur is not her thing. It doesn't make her sick. It is just a matter of preference. But here she is, my Liza, conceding to have a drink with me. She puts the second glass and the bottle down next to me, and she walks around the pool, as the small pool's stairs are across from me. She allows the robe to fall from her shoulders, revealing that she is wearing a bikini. A purple bikini with tied bottoms. She turns to take the robe to the chair, which I think is just so that I see that the bottoms are barely covering anything in the back. Liza has never worn a bikini for as long as I have known her. She has always covered up. I am not complaining, but now I am curious about where she got this, considering our current circumstances.

She turns around to face me, and then she lets her hair out of its puff, and the curls of her natural hair fall along her shoulders, and I moan to myself. She walks into the water slowly, keeping her eyes on me the entire time. I feel like I am in a trance, watching her descent. She gets to me, and then instead of sitting next to me, she puts her hands on my shoulders and straddles me. Who is this woman, and what has she done with my wife? Liza is not the initiator, ever. Again, I am not complaining, just taking notice.

First, she straddles me loosely. Then she moves snugly against me, so much that our groins are now right on top of each other. As much as I was slightly hard before she came out here, I am entirely on fire and erect now. She reaches up to pull my locs out of the loc bun they are in. I don't really like getting my locs wet in the pool. They are hard to wash alone. So usually, I wait to get my hair washed at my loc shop. Liza knows this, but she reaches up to pull them down all the same. I reach up and grab her arm to stop her.

She looks me in the eyes, and with a sultry voice, she says, "I will wash them." She waits for my nod of acquiescing. I really wasn't going to say no, because right now, the question going through my mind is, *what is she up to.* As she looks back up to undo my bun, I see that on the side of one of the triangular bikini tops barely covering those breasts I love, there is a small cursive gold embroidery, which says Poweress. *Oh, they set us up, for real,* is my thought.

She finally figures out how to undo the bun, and my long locs fall down my shoulders, landing in the water in front and behind me. She runs her fingers through my locs and starts to massage my scalp just as she begins to move her hips in a grind against my hardened member. I dip my head low, reposition my lower half for better grind access, and let her have at it.

The feel of her fingers is so relaxing and intimate, and the rotation of her hips is building passion within me. I don't know how long she massages both of my heads, but eventually, she stops, and she leans over and picks up the glass of Henny she poured for herself, and she takes a drink. I watch her wince and shake when the liqueur hits her throat, and I smirk. I throw back the rest of my second glass, and then I put my glass down, just as she is taking another sip. Then she kisses me. She allows what is left of the amber liquid to flow from her mouth to mine. The liqueur mixed with the sweet taste of Liza has me moaning as she kisses me deeply. Then she does something I would have never thought she would do, she steps back, and she unties every tie on her bikini until she is birthday suit naked before me. I am up so fast, removing my swim trunks. I splash water everywhere. She laughs at me and then walks back to me and sits right on my erection, gliding up and down its length, and riding me until we are both moaning in passion and bursting with climatic ecstasy.

****

After round two in the pool, yes, another position was warranted. She is sitting in my arms on the lounge chair with her back against my front. It is so peaceful. She draws circles on my forearm as we look out at the lake and the moon. We are both lost in our own private thoughts.

Then, in that sultry voice she has had all night, she asks, "Do you want to talk about it?"

I know I can say no, and she will leave it alone. But, I know I should go ahead. After all, I am supposed to be trying to be honest with myself and transparent with her. I adjust myself in the seat, and she moves to turn around, but I stop her. I need to do this in our current position. I feel safe like this.

I play with the curls in her hair for a few minutes, and then I take a deep breath, "When I was seven years old, I was in the second grade. We had this project where we were supposed to look at our parents and write down what about us looked like them. You know, the I get my eyes from my dad and so on kind of project. I remember being so excited to do the project because we got to also bring a picture of our family to school for show and tell. I got home, and Mom and Dad were at a meeting, so the nanny was there with Christy. Christy had to be about three or four years old, which means she had gotten home from preschool before me. I remember running up to our nanny, Ms. Trish, and telling her all about my project as I helped her fix snacks. I told her I wanted to do it with Dad, so I was going to wait for him. Ms. Trish called him to let him know. He came home early from the meeting to help me. He never came home early." I could hear the excitement in my own voice. "When he came home, Christy went to sleep, and Ms. Trish did too. Dad took me to his study, and he pulled out the latest family picture. I pulled out my instruction paper from my backpack, and we sat down together at his desk. I used to love sitting at his desk with him. I stared at the picture and started saying the things that I got from whom. As I kept going, I realized everything on my paper was about Dad and Christy. I recall looking at his face while I realized this. Like any 7-year-old, I had said it out loud. My Dad's face tensed, and he wouldn't look at me. So, I finally said, 'Dad, what did I get from Mom?' He didn't say anything, just got up and got a drink from his cabinet."

I pause in my story and let the visual of that moment play in my head. He was so tense and anxious. He couldn't even make eye contact with me. "I had to ask him five times before he turned around and sat down. I will never forget the look on his face that night. There were tears in his eyes. I had asked him what was wrong, and then he grabbed my hand and said words that shattered me. 'Son, Lady LeBlanc is not your Mother. She did not give birth to you.'" I feel Liza tense beneath me and hug my arm closer, but she says nothing. She knows I need silence to finish. After a breath, I continued, "I asked what a few times before he told me his story. Come to find out; my Father was in love with another woman before he and Lady LeBlanc got married. The other woman was my Mother. The problem was my Father's family wanted him to continue the legacy they had started, so marrying Lady LeBlanc, Antonia is her name. I don't really say her given name much." I paused and let that thought sit within me and then continued. "My grandparents wanted my Father and Antonia to marry to keep the two highest-ranking families in the Order at the top. As you know, the higher you are ranked, the more the family is paid annually. Anyway, my Father decided he would do what they wanted. At the time, he and Antonia were friends, and they knew each other well because they had grown up together. They understood each other. My Father broke things off with my Mother the day before his wedding. Supposedly, my Mother knew it was coming, and they just waited until there was no more time to end it. After about six months, my Father was notified by a mutual friend that he had seen my Mother in the store, and she was pregnant. At that, my Father sought my Mother out, and sure enough, she was pregnant with me. Ms. Trish eventually told me that my Father wanted to have both families, but Antonia said no. This made my Father have to go back and forward between households to ensure I knew him, even if that meant traveling between cities. My Father told me that when I was two years old, my

Mother died from complications with some type of autoimmune disease. He then brought me home to live with him and Antonia. Antonia had said that in order for me to stay with them, we needed to never speak of my Mother again, that I needed to see her as my Mother. No one was to know that I was not their child. At the time of all this, my family lived in Atlanta as my Father was doing a visiting professorship, something he did off and on. This meant that the members of the Order, except my grandparents on all sides, had no idea that I even existed. As my parents had done a good job of keeping my paternity hidden in New Orleans. Therefore, it was easy for my Father and Antonia to return to New Orleans and pretend that they had had a child while they were gone. My Father had to pretend my Mother did not exist. Of course, at two years old, I eventually called Antonia 'Mom', and I forgot about my Mother, as there were no pictures of my Mother anywhere. However, at seven years old, in that office with my Dad, he pulled out his wallet, went into a hidden pocket, and pulled out an old picture. Before he even told me who it was, I knew. I remembered her eyes, which looked so much like mine, and her heart-shaped lips, like yours." I didn't realize I was crying until I sniffled. Liza let me cry without turning around, again accepting my slight privacy. "I remember thinking that she was the most beautiful woman I had ever seen. He gave me the photo, and I held it in my hand and just stared at her. At that moment, I was so confused and excited. My Father just sat there looking at me, looking at the picture for I don't know how long. Eventually, he took the picture back. I asked him if I could keep it. He told me no. Then he broke my heart. He told me that I could never speak of that moment or my birth Mother again. I was never to ask questions about her, and I was by no means to tell Antonia that I knew. I pleaded with him, and I was crying on the floor. It felt like he was taking my Mother away, even though I only had seen a picture. Then he said with the coldest look and the coldest voice that I have ever seen or heard on him even to this day, 'Olivier absolutely by no means should you ever cry. No Son of Mine is allowed to cry like some little girl. Get up.' He yanked me off the floor and continued, 'That woman does not exist. This family is all you have.' When I told him I did not feel that way, he responded, 'your feelings and opinions do not matter here. You do as you are told and keep your thoughts, feelings, and opinions to yourself.' Then he straightened me up, poked out my chest, and said, 'today, you are older and stronger. No baby nonsense.' He looked me in the eye, and I knew he meant all he said. At that moment, I decided I would never share my real thoughts, feelings, and opinions with him or anyone else again. From that moment, I went with their flow, joined what they wanted, and went to the schools they wanted until I was 21 and decided I didn't want to play by their rules. So, I went into singing. During that time, I learned that Antonia hated my singing not just because it was not a plan but because my birth Mother was a singer. I was sent a tape of her singing, and she sounded more beautiful, angelic, and soulful than anyone I have ever heard. I could never figure out who sent it to me, it came my senior year of college, and it is why I chose to sing for a while." I took a breath. I could hear her sniffling. She is crying for me, just as she has done so many times with my family. I rub her shoulders and continue. "My honesty is that I have never really been allowed to be me. I have never allowed myself to fully do what I want most in the world because every time I think about this, I feel like that hopeless 7-year-old in my Father's study. There is no way for me to know what I want to know about my Mother and her side of the family. The older I get, I realize how much like her I must be because when I watch my family, there are so many things that don't fit me. I look like my Father, but I am not a pushover. I don't enjoy this place of beating to someone else's drum. I want to be free to beat to my own drum. The shop gives me some of that, but I hold back for their sake, and I know it."

Liza turns around and faces me head-on. She looks me in the eyes as I continue, "I know you will be fine with me pursuing this. You are always pushing me to follow my heart. I don't think I have the strength to face this alone, to go at this alone. What if what I find is worse than what I have? What if my Mother was a horrible person, and that is the real reason he left her?" I shake my head and look at my lap. Then I feel Liza's hands on my face and her lips on my forehead. She lifts my head so that my eyes meet hers.

I feel the tears in my eyes as I look at the tears in hers. In a soft, calming voice laced with so much love, she says, "Olivier, you are not alone. I will help you. Don't let the what-ifs stop you from knowing the truth. Your Mother had to be wonderful because all of the things that I love about you are the exact things that make you different from everyone in your family. Yes, you have their determination and grit, but you also have this sense of resolve about what you want and who you love. You stand up for what you really want and who you really love, and as much as you don't share all of your thoughts, you do share some with me. Olivier, you are not that 7-year-old boy anymore. You are not helpless or hopeless." She takes a breath and wipes my tears. Then she wipes her own. "I am so sorry that your Father did that to you. I can't begin to imagine how you have handled all this for this long. But Baby, please don't carry this by yourself anymore. Let me carry it with you. Then, when you are ready, we can eventually release it to God because He is the only one that can heal the deep hurt you carry." With that, she climbs into my lap and hugs me close, and for the first time since that night, I allow myself to cry out all of my pain and frustration on her shoulder and into her neck.

Chapter 12: Liza

Six months later

That last night at the retreat was heartbreaking, but things have been excellent since then. Olivier did speak with the Order about me helping with his duties, but with all that it entailed, we decided that he would finish off with what we owed them. In two months, he will be free to step back from his official position if he wants to. However, I think he is starting to enjoy the Order again. Honestly, I would be okay if he chose to stay because he wanted to be there versus him having to be there. We will see.

We also decided to sign the kids up for carpool. Now our 12-year-old twins, Trevor and Alisha, ride with a group of friends to school, and the Lex and Sydney ride with the neighbors. Of course, like most carpools, we have a week to take all the kids. However, this means I am free for two weeks of the month to not worry about taking the kids to school, and Olivier now picks them up every other week as well. This has helped with stress, and it gives me much-needed time to either work or to take time off.

I also did something I never do. I invited Olivier to come with me to an event with the girls three months ago. Jackson, my friend Trina's husband, was awarded businessman of the year. Usually, I would have gone to the event alone as my time with the girls. Whether the girls' husbands were there or not, my activities with the girls are my time away from home, aka the kids and Olivier, and my time to decompress. Now, however, I feel like Olivier, and I are moving in the right direction, so I invited him. Of course, the girls fell all over themselves when they saw us. I thought I was going to have to knock a heffa out with the way they were drooling all over my husband. However, I understood because my husband was looking extra sexy that night. Plus, they hadn't seen Olivier in a long while. The girls were all crazy about my dress as well. It was mermaid-style, and it definitely showed a little more skin and curves than my usual conservative attire.

With the extra time, I have due to the changes Olivier and I have made with the kids and my decision to delegate more tasks out at work, I decided to start going to the gym to tone up, not lose weight. I realized at the retreat that my husband actually likes my thickness, and to be honest, so do I. Therefore, toning it up and making it flexible is the goal these days. Anyway, with my new regimen, I feel incredibly sexy. Needless to say, I am feelin' myself, singing that Nikki Minaj and Beyonce song from a while back. With this feeling in mind, I decided I wanted to change my wardrobe. I want to change this whole conservative look I have gotten myself into. The retreat helped me to realize that I needed to really be me. When we left, I started doing it piece by piece, being honest about needing help with the kids, being honest about not trying to control everything at work, and choosing not to be a perfectionist. I realized the true me is ok with a little chaos. Everything does not have to be picture-perfect all the time. It is ok that the house is not spotless every day, I don't want it to be a disaster, but I do want it to look like a home and not a picture from the inside of a home décor magazine. I also realized that this whole conservative persona of mine has gone on long enough. I know my parents are perfectionists and the epitome of conservativeness. The entire southern bell situation. However, in reality, that is not me. I have changed a lot over the last six months, but now it is time to stop giving myself small makeovers and go all the way out. I am ready to make myself over. I am prepared for the real me to shine through and not just peek out.

With this in mind, I decided to send a group text to my besties, Lyric, Trina, and Erica. It is time for reinforcements.

Hey Ladies!! So I have a request. I know we are to do Label Ladies next month, but what if we change it up. I was thinking, would you guys mind helping give me a makeover??

While I am trying to decide what else I want to say, they start texting me.

Trina: **WTF!! Hell Yeah!!**

Lyric: **Absolutely!!**

Erica: **How far are we talking??**

I love how all of us are so different. Trina is always the life of the party, and her being married has not dimmed that at all. If anything, Jackson brings it out more. He lets her be herself, and he backs her up. It is crazy how much alike they are and how their love has blossomed into such a fantastic thing. None of us would have thought that their one-night stand personalities would have led to such a wonderful marriage and beautiful baby on the way.

Lyric has been my ride or die since we were kids. She used to have my back on the playground and in private with my panic attacks. I am so happy I have not had one of those in years. Knock on wood. Anyway, Lyric and I were not as close during college since she was in Atlanta, but when I got to Atlanta for grad school, it was like no time had passed. She is the one who introduced me to the other girls. Even during undergrad, I knew if I really needed Lyric, she would be right there. As I said, she is my ride or die, and I am hers. It is funny that even though she got married after me, her love for Ezekiel makes me want to love my husband more and better. To this day, Lyric and Ezekiel share a fantastic bond. Yes, they have their struggles, and she calls me for advice since I am like the marriage OG of the group. However, at the end of the day, love prevails. I am just so glad I get to watch their love grow.

Erica, my poor Erica. Don't get me wrong. She is not my poor Erica because she is still single. It takes a married person who has been married as long as I have to say genuinely there is something beautiful about singleness. In your singleness, there is a time of truth with yourself and God that you don't have when you are married. As a married person, as much as life is still about you and God, it is also about you, God, and your husband. Do not get me wrong. Marriage is a beautiful thing. Trust me, it is, but I have learned that we should find our happiness and peace in every season of life. We have to be content where God has us. That being said, Erica knows who she is, but she doesn't think that it is enough for a man. This means that men tend to not think she is enough, either. We keep trying to show her that she has to be confident in herself and believe she is enough, and then others will think so too. We have told her this for years, but she keeps on keeping on. One day she will get it. I hope and pray she will.

Ok, now I need to text back. *How far do I want to go with this makeover?* I think about how when we usually have our Label Ladies brunches, we eat in the garden and wear the same name-brand clothes. It was Trina's idea because she likes name brands. Anyway, it is fun. However, when I think about it, I am always the most covered up. When I think about college with Christy, she would have to beg me to wear things that showed a little cleavage and leg. I realize I have never really just been free in my dress. Even as a kid, my mother would pick out things with high collars and pants suits. Since she dressed that way, I just went with what she did. I mean, she was the most successful woman I knew at the time. I think about how nothing I own except for some gifts from Olivier and some recent purchases makes me happy when I put it on. I don't put on my clothes and feel beautiful and alive. They are functional and fashionable, but still just functional. With that in mind, I send my text.

I want to go all the way. Hair, make-up, clothes, shoes. I want a whole new wardrobe. I want to live in my clothes. But I want y'all to shop for you too, of course.

Lyric: **Absolutely, Boo!! Let's make you shine from crown to toe.**

Trina: **Of course, we are shopping for us too. You know I can't help myself, pregnant or not. Lol**

Erica: **Let's do this!! We should meet earlier though, so we have more time.**

Me: **I agree. What about we meet at the mall at 10:30a?**

Trina: **Bet. Galleria?**

Lyric: **Of Course, Ole' Boogie One!**

Me: **You know you are not that much better, right?**

Erica: **Oh please, we all got tendencies. LOL.**

Trina, Me, Lyric: **Absolutely!!**

Me: **Thank you, Ladies. I can't wait. See you next month!!**

Trina: **One month to D-Day!!**

Lyric: **I need to go check my money. See y'all!**

Erica: **See y'all!**

We each sent a purple heart emoji which is our customary end of conversation confirmation. To say I am excited is an understatement. Next month's Label Ladies will be the best.

****

I check on the roast in the slow cooker and then go into the refrigerator to decide what vegetables I will be making for dinner. As I am browsing, Anya comes from upstairs. She is our housekeeper, another addition to my efforts at delegating tasks. Hey, the Proverbs 31 woman had assistance. It was time that I got some too.

"Hey, Ms. LeBlanc. We are finished for today. Are you okay with keeping your cleanings at every two weeks? You asked me to remind you for us to talk on this visit."

I turn around and see Anya's smiling face. She is a beautiful mocha woman, and I love that she owns the cleaning agency we use. Lyric hooked me up with her.

I smile slightly. "I think every two weeks is good. Let's make it the works every two weeks. I noticed the kids seemed to mess up everything. With all of their after-school activities this year, I am sure this place will be a mess. Will that work, or do I need to switch to weekly to ensure everything is done?"

She is shaking her head before I finish, "Honestly, we can do it every two weeks, but I don't think you need everything, even with the kids being so busy. Some of the things. How about I send you a recommendation on what will probably need to be cleaned based on what we regularly see. Then I will send you the price choice between everything and a modified recommendation? Do you think that will work?"

"Yes! See you are the best. Ok, get it to me this week coming, and on your next visit, we will switch to whatever is decided." I hug her and thank her for her service as I hand her the tip for this visit.

As she goes out of the door, I hear her speak to someone. I know exactly who she is talking to, my mother. I know that voice anywhere. My mother never just drops by, so this should be an interesting visit. I look at the time and see that it is 3p, which means I have about 2 hours before the kids arrive as Olivier agreed to take them to get ice cream to celebrate the fact that they all got good grades on their report cards. Our children's report cards get emailed to us the morning of report card day, which means we know their grades before they do since they don't get report cards until the end of the day.

"Oh, Honey, this place looks amazing." My mother says as she hugs me close and then sits at the bar across from me. She watches me for a minute as I start prepping veggies to be roasted in about an hour or two.

"Hello, Mother. How are you?" I say as I prep.

"I am good. You look great. It has been a minute since we have seen each other?"

"Mother, it has been a little over a month. You know getting everyone back to school is always a busy time."

"You can't tell with how nice everything looks. When did you get a housekeeper?"

I shake my head. Here she goes, "About three months ago. I told you I was starting to delegate."

"Yes, at work. A great leader always delegates at work but keeps their hands on things at home. You are the wife here; it is your job to make it all work here."

"I appreciate the advice, Mother. So. what brings you by?" I say, trying to get off of this subject. I realized months ago that I did everything because I was still working from my mother's view that I needed to be a Proverbs 31 woman. Who supposedly did everything. However, when I read the scripture and listened to God's revelation, I realized that, yes, she managed everything. However, Sis had help. It was time I stopped trying to live up to my mother's view and made my own. Plus, when I was growing up, I had a nanny who picked me up from school and watched me at the lab. So, even my mother had help. I shake the thoughts from my mind as my mother begins to speak again.

"Well, I figured since you were not coming to see us. I would come to you."

"Sorry, I know I usually visit y'all's office once a month, but I have just been busy. How are you?"

"Good." That tone was loaded.

"How is Father?" I say with a smile, trying to change topics again.

"Missing you." *Oh, so, no dodging this one*, I think to myself.

I stop cutting the veggies, and I look up at my mother. I look so much like her. The only difference is her toffee skin versus my ivory-colored skin. I got my color from my father. "Mom, what is it?" I give her my undivided attention. I know that is what she wants.

"We want you to finally come work at the family business so that we can start making moves to retire."

"Mother, that is not happening. I am not that kind of chemist. "

"Well, become that kind of chemist. If you come now, we can train you. You are smarter than this cosmetics world you have gotten into."

"Mother, I appreciate that, I do. However, I will tell you as I did the last time we had this conversation. I love the chemistry of cosmetics. The dimensions and intricacies. I love that when women put on what I created, they feel beautiful. I love what I do."

"But it is not the same as pharmaceuticals. You could save lives and cure diseases. You could change the world, not just someone's face. When we sent you to get your Ph.D., you know, and you agreed that you were coming to work at Legacy Pharmaceuticals and step into your place as a Monroe."

"Mother, I understand your position, and, yes, I thought I was going to do that too. I fell in love with another branch of chemistry. Mother, it was not intentional. It has been years. Why are you still pushing this?"

"Elizabeth," *oh man, I am in trouble now.* I tell myself. Not only did she use my given name, but she was also giving me that black mother voice. You know that tone that tells you they are no longer playing with you. "Why do you insist on being subordinate? We did not raise you this way. You are a Monroe, and a Monroe will sit as CEO of Legacy, and that is final."

I take a breath. I go back to prepping my sides for dinner. I decide on potatoes to go along with the veggies. The aggression I am feeling now makes me want to make mash potatoes from scratch so I can smash something. I take out the potatoes and peel the skin.

"Elizabeth Monroe, are you going to keep ignoring me?" She raises her voice at me, another sign this is going downhill. I hear the back door open; shoot, Olivier is early.

Trevor comes in first. He is my oldest. My beautiful twins, Trevor and Alisha, were born seven minutes apart, and Trevor ensures no one ever forgets it.

"Hey, Mom." He gives me a hug. "Grandmother, hey." He says, waving at her.

"Honey, hey is for horses." He looks at me. I shake my head like pay her no mind. He says, "Right. Hello, Grandmother. It is a pleasure as always." Then he gives her a nod.

I chuckle because I know he is being sarcastic and dramatic, but she doesn't even catch it since she smiles happily at him. He looks at me and smiles, and he goes upstairs.

Next to enter are Lex and Syndey. Lex was my second pregnancy, and he is ten years old. Syndey is my baby, and she is seven. As they enter, they say, "Mommy, we did well on our report cards!!" I give them both big hugs and kiss on their foreheads. "Yes, y'all did!! I am so proud of you."

"Thanks, Mommy. Can we play video games after we clean up?" Lex asks.

"Sure. I am sure Daddy wants to play too."

"We are going to beat him big time," Syndey says as she makes karate moves. Mortal Kombat is their game of choice. Actually, all of us love that game. To say that game night gets intense is an understatement of significant proportions.

"Well, I am sure that you both have homework you could be doing instead of playing games." My mother says. They both turn slowly. It is so hilarious. It is as if they didn't even see her. They look at me and then at her. I nod, like go ahead.

They turn to her. Lex states, "Actually no, Grandmother. We finished all of our homework at school. So, we are free to play."

"Play? Well, playing is not learning." My mother says.

I see both of their faces make the look that Olivier does when he is about to go off. I put my hands on their shoulders and say directly to my mother, "Actually, play is learning. They are still at the age where playing is as important as everything else. It allows them to process. Plus, they are doing well with their assignments. We don't mind letting them have a little fun." I look at the kids and pat them on the back to say run along before she starts again.

As they run upstairs, Alisha comes in. I can tell she has been crying.

She runs into my arms and sobs. I hold her for a few minutes stroking her hair softly. Since she has my color, her emotions are showing in how red she has turned. Olivier comes in. Alisha looks at him like he is a trader, and then she runs upstairs.

"Alisha, Sweetie," I call after her. She keeps running. I turn to Olivier as he walks up to me, hugs me tightly, and gives me a nice, slow kiss.

"Hey, Belle."

"Hello, Olivier." He kisses my forehead, and then he turns to my mother.

"Mother Monroe, what a surprise." He walks over to her and kisses the back of her hand.

She blushes slightly and then bats her eyes at him. From the moment they met, he has always been able to charm her.

I remember when I was in college, and I was getting inducted into the chemistry honor society. For my parents, this was one of my greatest achievements because it meant I would be offered a great spot in any of the major Ph.D. programs I had applied to. I remember being a senior, and it was Mardi Gras. After the ceremony, I came off the stage from taking our group photo. My parents were waiting on the side of the stage. I hugged them and showed them the award and the pin. Then Christy walked up and tapped my shoulder. I turned and hugged her close. I was so surprised she was there because she had been busy with a research project that had taken her out of town. She was not due back until my graduation, but my friend made it happen. Then she nodded to the right for me to look. When I looked, there was Olivier looking every bit of the sexy man that he was. He was still dressed in his performance black leather jacket and a black shirt with a pair of fitted black jeans. He had on purple suede timberlands. He was coming from a show earlier in the day.

He strolled toward me, and his swagger was terrific. I was dripping between my legs like no one's business. He always affected me, and that day was no different. At this point, we were dating, and it was serious. We had not said the I love you part yet, and we had not even had sex yet, but I knew deep down he would make sure I was good no matter what. He always made sure I was good. When Christy decided to move out and move in with her boyfriend. Olivier actually paid my bills. My parents wanted me to live on campus or in an apartment that they would have access to whenever, and I did not want that. So, they said they would not pay for my room and board otherwise. When I told Olivier, I was crying and devastated because I had no way to pay for where I was living with Christy without her. I didn't tell Christy because I wanted her to be happy, but her moving meant I had to go back to the dorms or give my parents access to my entire life. Olivier said, "Absolutely not." He started paying my bills and buying my food immediately.

Anyway, we were a couple. I could tell he was cautious with me, though I was unsure why. At the ceremony, He walked up to me and kissed my nose and then my forehead like he always did. He hugged me close and told me congratulations.

"Olivier, what are you doing here? You have a gig tonight." I smiled up at him.

"Celebrating you is more important than a gig. I canceled." I smiled broader and threw my arms around him. I felt his deep chuckle vibrating against me.

Then my father cleared his throat. I pulled back from Olivier, but I stared into his eyes. I had completely forgotten about my parents, which was another effect of being in Olivier's presence. Whenever he was around, I seemed to lose track of time and people. I actually loved getting lost in him. It was easy, simple, and natural. It didn't require me to think or analyze. I could just be and trust that he would catch me if I fell, and vice versa.

My father cleared his throat again. I turned around. My father was reddening in the face. My mother looked pissed. Monroe ladies did not show that kind of affection in public, and here I was.

"Mother and Father, you remember Christy?" I turned to Christy, and she shook their hands.

"Of course, Dear. How are you, Christy? How is that master's program coming?" My father said.

"Almost done, Sir. It is a pleasure to see you both again."

"It is really nice to see you too, Honey." My mother said.

My mother then looked back at me and made a point of looking at Olivier.

"Father, Mother, this is Olivier. He is Christy's brother and my boyfriend." The last part, I said, smiling up at him. He smiled down at me and then turned his attention to my parents. Since he was still holding my hand, he reached out to shake my mother and father's hands with his free hand.

"Ms. Monroe, it is truly an honor to meet you. Liza speaks so highly of you, and your beauty speaks to how Liza became so beautiful." He took her hand and kissed the back of it. Oh, he was good. My mother blushed and became all coy.

"Mr. Monroe, it is my pleasure to finally meet the man who has taught Liza so much. Meeting the man in her life is a gift, as I know, she does not share you with most." He shakes his hand firmly. My father sizes him up. He stares him down, and Olivier does not waver at all. My father likes that in a man. He nods at Olivier.

"Olivier, is it?"

"Yes, Sir."

"I think you should join us for dinner. I am sure there is a lot to discuss. As you said, my Elizabeth does not introduce just anyone to us."

"Of course. I would love to."

I smile and shake my head.

"Christy, you should come too." I turned to her and offered. She is shaking her head no before I finish.

"Sorry, I can't. I have to go back to Chicago for the presentation tomorrow. I just wanted to come. I will call you."

"Ok, girl. Thank you so much for coming." We hug each other, and Olivier walks her out.

That night my parents fell in love with Olivier. He charmed them to no end. They even allowed him to escort me home at the end of the night, and they went back to their hotel. We were to meet them in the morning. That night Olivier took me home. He walked me in as he always did.

"Hey, do you need anything?" He said, leaning on my marble bar top as I got some water.

"Like what?" I turn to him.

"Like food, money, anything."

"No, I am ok." I take a drink. "Thank you for coming tonight. I know Mardi Gras is a big season for you."

"You don't have to thank me for caring about you."

I smirked at him. He stared deeply into my eyes. It was so intense I eventually broke eye contact. I knew a blush was rising up my neck because I could feel the heat. I looked at the floor. He stared more.

"Elizabeth, what do you want from us?"

I looked up at him, and he was serious. "What do you mean?"

"Exactly what I said. Liza, what do you want?"

I leaned against the counter and stared at him. What did I want from us? Up until he asked me, I was just going with the flow. I didn't allow myself to think past the present moment. I don't know if it was because I wasn't ready for the answer or if I saw no future with us.

He smiled at me, "You don't know."

"It is not that I don't want anything. I guess I have just been going with the flow. What do you want from us?"

He looked at me, "Honestly?"

"Of course."

"Forever." He rounded the bar and came to stand right in front of me. I must be losing my mind was the thought going through my head. He didn't just say that, did he?

As if reading my mind, he took my hands in his, and then he gave me that look that said I want to provide you with the world. A look that had been appearing more and more on his face. "Elizabeth Monore, I want forever with you." Then he dropped to one knee. My hands flew to my mouth. Oh, My Gaud!!

"Liza, from the moment I met you, I knew that you would change my life. I wanted to break the rules, make new rules, and do whatever it would take to make that blush rise up your neck every day of my life. I love the woman you are. I love how you take care of me and how you allow me to take care of you. I love how you support me and build me. How you fight for what you want and go with the flow when you need or want to. Liza, I love you. I am so in love with you."

I felt the tears rolling down my cheeks as he shared his love with me. I was lost in his eyes, in his words, and in him. He continued.

"Liza, I wanted to wait to tell you I loved you until I knew for sure. Belle, I know for sure and then some." He dug in his pocket, and out came a ring box. "I am so sure that I am in love with you and want to share forever with you that I ask you this day, Elizabeth Monroe, do you want forever with me? Will you give me the honor and pleasure of becoming my wife?" With that, he opened the ring box. A gorgeous pear-shaped pink 3-carat diamond set in rose gold stared back at me. It was perfect in its clarity, rarity, and size. The tears fell from my eyes even more. I looked into those cognac pools he called eyes, and what I saw was pure love. I knew my answer.

"Yes, I want to have forever with you. I want to be your wife."

With that, he slid the ring onto my finger. He stood and kissed me thoroughly.

****

Present Moment

I must have been smiling because when I came to, Olivier was chuckling, and my mother had a scowl on her face. I shook my head to clear my thoughts.

"Belle, what were you thinking about?" Olivier is standing next to me.

"The first time that you met my parents." I smile at him. He gives me a knowing look. We got engaged that night, but we didn't share our engagement until my graduation. So, everyone thinks we got engaged at my graduation. It's funny because we still had not been physically intimate even with the engagement, but that's a memory for another day. I shake my head again.

"So, why was Alisha crying, Olivier?" I turn to him. The smile that was on his face a moment before is now gone. He leans against the countertop and looks at me.

"Probably some boy. You know that when you don't keep your children occupied with schoolwork, they find other things or people to occupy their time or body."

I glare at my mother, "Mother, that is not called for. My children are well-balanced. I understand you disagree with how we are handling their work; however, sitting here making disrespectful remarks is not called for." I turn back to Olivier. "What is going on?"

"She asked if she could have a boyfriend."

"See, told you. Occupied." My mother interrupts.

Olivier and I both take a breath. "She likes the boy on her co-ed volleyball team, Luther, Duke, something,"

"Luke is his name." I offer up.

"Yeah, him. He asked her to go to dinner with him on a date. She asked me, and I said no."

I arch an eyebrow in return.

"You didn't even ask Liza?" My mother interrupts again.

"Mother, please."

"Well, we have an agreement. The kids can't date alone until they are 15 years old, and at 13 years old, maybe some supervised dates."

"Oh."

I shake my head. She is always trying to insert herself into our business. I shake my head at my mother and then look at Olivier.

"What?" He is getting defensive. "We said no dating, or did you change your mind?"

"No, I didn't. We said no dating, and our agreement stands, but we have not said it to the kids. So did you explain it to her so that she knows? It is not that you don't want her to date ever or that you are being cold, but that we think it is best because..." I state gently.

He takes a breath and runs his hand down his face. "I didn't think to do that."

"I don't see why you need to. We didn't do that, Liza."

"That is exactly why I know we should," I say, cutting my eyes at my mother.

"Olivier, go wash up. I will put the vegetables into the oven to roast, and then we can talk to her together. Honestly, we may need to have the same conversation with Trevor."

"You are right." He kisses my nose and then my forehead. "Give me about 30 minutes, and we can talk to them."

He kisses my mother on the cheek and goes to our bedroom on the other side of the living room.

I turn to my mother and see she is watching Olivier leave. I promise, if she were not an old lady, she would probably be trying to talk to my man. I shake my head.

"Mother, are you staying for dinner?"

"I would love to. Should I call your Father?"

I look at the time and see that he should be getting off soon. I know she would have cooked if she was not here, so I say, "Sure. Tell him it will be ready in an hour."

With that, I send Olivier a text letting him know my parents are staying for dinner. He says ok, which I knew he would. Then I season the veggies, put them in the oven, and start boiling the potatoes.

Chapter 13: Liza

A Month Later

The day has finally arrived. Make-Over Day!!! My parents picked up all of the kids. Yes, all four of them. I was surprised. I told my mother that I was going to do a make-over on myself, and to my astonishment, she was excited. My mother has always been the one that liked things to stay the same. She thought that you pick a career and invent yourself once in life. Now that she and my father are working toward retirement, I think some of her past mindsets have changed, like this make-over. The conversation was interesting and supportive, even, which was another surprise.

"Mother, I am going to go do a make-over soon. Just so you don't freak out when you see my new hair." I said to her.

To be honest, I am not sure why I told her. Well, let me stop lying. I think a part of me has always wanted my parents to be interested in me past my brain and how it works. Past the fact that I am so much like them in the analytical sense. Past the part that makes us good chemists. I wanted them to like me for my personality, my funny side, and my caring side, but I never got that. I was always praised for my accomplishments in school. You would think that that would have made me do worst since I wanted them to like other parts of me, but instead, it drove me to do better and fight harder. School accomplishments were the only way that my parents would see me. Therefore, it became the only way I saw myself. I went away for college in hopes that I would one day learn to love and like myself for things other than school. Slowly, it worked, but life tested that with kids, marriage, and everything else. However, I digress, back to the conversation with my mom about the make-over.

"Mother, I am going to go do a make-over soon. Just so you don't freak out when you see my new hair." I said to her.

"Really, Honey? Why?" Her voice didn't hold any judgment, which was new. I guess the counseling she just started was working.

"I think it is time for a change."

"OK. I just wanted to make sure it wasn't for Dante or us."

"Why would you think that?"

"Well, to be honest, I know that you used to be a lot freer after college, and you have slowly turned more conservative in the way you used to say you hated. Plus, I realize now through some very tough conversations that I may not have always been that supportive of you."

When she said that, I almost died. My mother never takes the fault. It is like Gabrielle Monroe could never make mistakes and do any wrong. I know she did make mistakes. We all do, but she would never admit it. I didn't say that, of course. Instead, I remained quiet.

"Honey, I want you to be happy. So, if this make-over will do that, then go for it."

"Seriously?"

"Yes. I love you....... In fact, is there anything I can do to help?"

Shocked, I was silent for a while, staring at my phone.

"Elizabeth? Honey, did I lose you?"

"No, I am here. I was just a little stunned."

"I am a work in progress, Honey. Now, come on. How can I help?"

"Well, can you watch Lex and Sydney next weekend, and I will ask Olivier's parents to watch Trevor and Alisha?"

"No worries. Your Father and I will take them all. We were thinking of going to a resort near Dallas with an indoor water park. The kids will love it. I will check with your Father on times for pick-up and return. Ok?"

"Mother, are you sure? All of them? You know they can be a bit much."

"Elizabeth, I may have been a Mother of one, but I am the Big Sister to four. I am sure that the kids will be taken care of between your Father and me."

"Ok......That sounds perfect. Let me know when you guys will come....... And Mom, thank you for this."

"No problem, Honey...... Well, let me go. Duke just came downstairs. We are headed to the movie. His choice. Can you believe your Father wants to go to the movie? To see Batman?"

"Batman? Dad never likes movies, just documentaries."

"Times are changing. Talk to you later. Love you."

"Yes, they are." She didn't hear my agreement as she had already hung up.

That was the conversation we had last weekend, and my parents came and picked up the kids yesterday evening. Now, here I am, this Saturday at 6 am, drinking coffee while sitting on the back patio swing. I am a little nervous; I will be honest about that. It was my idea for this make-over, and I know that my friends will make sure I look good, but I feel like this is the becoming of the new Liza. It is as if I have done all the inner work, and now it is time to let it show not just in my action but in my appearance.

"God, I thank you for this journey of honesty and discovery. Thank you for not letting me get comfortable with the way things were or letting me drown in that place. Thank you for knowing what I needed and providing it. Thank you for the changes in my parents and in their expression of love toward me. Thank you for Olivier and his love and his kind heart. Help me to be a better helpmate to him. Help him become the man of God that you intended for him to be. Strengthen him and guide him. Help us love and respect each other and continue in honesty and love on this journey of marriage and parenthood that you have provided. I am so grateful. I love you. In Jesus' name, Amen."

I wiped the tears that had started trickling down my cheeks as I said my prayer of gratitude. Then I hear the back door open and feel Olivier watching me. He says nothing for a while. Then he comes around and sits next to me. He takes my cup from my hand, puts it on the side table, and pulls me to rest against him with me laying between his legs. It is peaceful, and I do not feel the need to talk. I just breathe in the essence of him as he breathes in the essence of me. I feel the bond between us and the positivity of hope for the future. It reminds me of our wedding night and how at peace I felt with him.

"Olivier, you didn't have to do all of this?"

"Of course, I did, You are my wife, and there is nothing more important to me than you knowing that I love and respect you. I know tonight means a lot, and I do not take it lightly."

"I am nervous, Olivier."

"I know. You are shaking....... Come here. Let's go sit on the patio."

We walked outside to the back of the house, we had rented in San Croix for our honeymoon. There were beautiful trees lining the way to our private beach. The water appeared as black as the night around us and the moon provided a spotlight on the swing that rested on the back patio. Olivier unzipped my dress, leaving me in my white corset and slip. I sat down on the swing and watched as he took off his jacket and unbuttoned his shirt, leaving his white undershirt exposed. Then he sat next to me, put his leg behind me, and pulled me between his legs with my back to his chest. He took down the bun in my freshly pressed hair and ran his fingers smoothly through my tresses. Then he took some deep breaths. He kissed my forehead and said, "Liza breathe with me." Together we took deep breaths. I felt at peace, laying in his arms and watching the moon.

Then he said, "Liza, we do not have to make love tonight. You know that, right?"

I nodded my head.

"I am truly content with this right here." He motioned to our bodies. As much as he said that, I could feel his erection on my lower back. He had restrained himself through the course of our dating relationship. We had done many things, but I could never go all the way. I don't know why. Maybe I was scared of what it would be like to be genuinely naked before someone, not just in the physical sense but in the emotional and spiritual sense. But, he is my husband now. There is no reason to be afraid. Olivier has always shown me he has got me in more ways than one. It is time I do the same.

So, I sat up and turned to him. He sat up too and looked into my eyes. He pulled me into his lap, causing me to straddle his waist, and he kissed me gently and intimately. It was like he was searching the depths of me for answers only my body could answer. I pulled back, and he released my lips.

"Olivier, I want to make love to you tonight. Please take care with me."

"Always, Belle. Always."

With that, we shared a smile, and he began to undo my corset.

That night was so amazing. The love we shared in the connecting of our bodies and souls took me to heights I could have never dreamed of. When I woke the next morning, I lay between his legs with my breast against his chest, his arms wrapped around me, and a blanket was shielding our naked *bodies as the sun rose and the patio swing swung us*

peacefully.

A decade and some change later, here we lay on this patio of ours in the swing that was built to mimic the swing in San Croix. There is no ocean in front of us, just the fountain that leads to my mini medivotion garden and the outdoor playground we had customized for the kids. I snuggle into Olivier a little more, and he wraps his arms around me.

"Belle, why are you out here so early?"

"I am nervous...... and excited about today. What are you doing up? I thought one of the employees was opening the shop today."

"One of them is. I felt you leave. When you stayed gone so long, I came to make sure you were good. Why were you crying?"

I sit up and turn to him. He sits up slightly and looks at me with those beautiful cognac eyes. "I was praying a prayer of thank you and gratitude to God for everything that has happened and for where we are. It makes me happy." He arches his eyebrow as if saying, 'and the tears.' "They were happy tears, Olivier. The last few years were rough. I feel like we are coming out and into better. You know?"

He pulls me into him, letting my legs straddle his waist, leaving me sitting in his lap. He smirks at me, "I agree, Belle. I agree." Then he leans in and kisses me passionately and intoxicatingly. I feel him consume me as he moves our clothes out the way and finds my entrance with his hardened erection. And right there, we make love, just like in San Croix.

Chapter 14: Olivier

Liza is getting ready for her make-over today. It is funny how nervous she is. I will not say that, of course. I would be lying if I did not say that I am excited too. I have seen the changes she has been making in finding and being honest with her new self, and it has been great. There are many pieces of her that I have missed as we started having kids and her career took off. The more children we had and the more into work we both became, the more stringent and rigid she became. It was like the planner of her chemistry brain never went off. Everything was so cut and dry, but now, I see my Belle starting to rise again. There are times when she is more curious and funny than she has been in the last few years. She is freer and more passionate. Even the kids have noticed. It will be interesting to see what this make-over brings.

Liza is not the only one that has been changing. I have noticed the shifting in me too. I don't feel the need to be on eggshells with her. It is like the more honest she became with herself and started making the needed adjustments, the more honest I could be with myself and make my adjustments. I did not need to be fixated on if she was okay, because she was. On that journey of honesty, I realized it was time to have this conversation with my dad about my birth mother. Since the kids are gone, Liza will be out, and my mother and Christy are busy with the event tonight, I decided today is the best time. So here goes. I pick up my phone and dial my father's phone number. He answers on the second ring as always.

"Dante, son, how are you?"

"I am good. How are you?"

"Not too bad. I just got finished grading some papers from this workshop I am doing."

"Oh, that's right! How has that been, getting back into teaching Dr. LeBlanc?"

"Stop, now you sound like Christy." I chuckle at his joke. "It has been good. But let us not pretend that is why you called me. Olivier, what is it?"

I take a deep breath. Whenever he calls me Olivier, it is his way of saying I know this is a serious conversation. So, here we go.

"Dad........." I cannot even get the words out. I stand and start pacing the floor of my home office. I feel seven years old again. It is frustrating. I am a grown man. *Come on, Dante, get your shit together.* I tell myself.

"Dante, did I lose you?"

"No, I am here." I take a breath. "Dad, we need to talk."

"About?"

"My Mother."

"Your Mother is at the Houston Club getting things ready for the annual Festival of Lights event."

"Not that, Mother."

I hear him sigh deeply.

"Olivier, we have discussed this before, and I told you we would never again." His voice has changed from his usual playful, light-hearted demeanor to cold.

"No, you said what you wanted, but you did not give me the answers I needed."

"Olivier, Son, nothing good can come of this."

"Yes, it can."

"What?"

"Closure and insight."

I hear him breathe. I cannot make him have this conversation with me, but I have to try.

"Dad, I need to know about her. Who she was, and what parts of me are from her? There is a piece of my history that I cannot fill on my own. I love you and Mom. I do, but there is a piece of me that has nothing to do with either of you. I need to know. Please…… one transparent conversation is all I am asking. Have it all out with me, and then we can let it rest, but you have to give me all the information for once."

I hear him pacing now. I know this is hard. After all, he promised his wife never to do the exact thing I am asking. However, I know that he knows I am right. It would be different if I were just like him. Then, I would not have some of these questions. But I am not just like him. I am more like her, of that I am sure.

He stops pacing. His voice is low, as if he is exhausted already. "One conversation, Dante. I will answer all of your questions and give you all the information I have………Son, I love you, but I can only do this once. I told you the promise I made. I do not like going back on my word."

"I know, and thank you."

"Come by the house now. I will get all things we need. Your Mother will be gone all day. We can talk and then go to the Festival. Bring your clothes. Ok?"

"OK. Thank you, Dad."

"See you in a bit."

I wipe my hand down my face. I feel Liza's eye on me before I turn around.

"You ok?" She asks gently. Then I turn to her, and she can see the strain on my face. She comes to me and pulls me close.

"What do you need, Olivier?"

"Just pray with me."

I pull her in closer, and I begin to pray. We pray that the conversation goes well and that I have some resolve when it is over, and that I understand myself better. We also pray for her make-over. At the end, we share a kiss. She asks me if I need her to come with me.

"No, I need to do this alone. Enjoy your time. We will talk when I get back from the Festival."

"Ok." She kisses me again, and off she goes.

Chapter 15: Liza

Leaving Olivier was hard. It is excellent that he is ready to finally push for that conversation with his dad, but I don't think he will be able to move forward as quickly as he thinks. Olivier is really good at partially processing things and then compartmentalizing them until a later time for the sake of getting things done. I pray that he can do that today.

Anyway, I left because he asked me to. He wants and needs to do this alone, and I will support that. "God give him strength and an open mind. Protect and keep him. Amen."

As I finish my prayer, I am pulling up to Jazzy Juice, a new black-owned cold-pressed juice and smoothie place. Since I got the ladies out for Label Ladies so early, I figured that the least I could do was bring smoothies and some delicious pastries. I pull on my two-tone black and tan moon Tory Burch crossbody that matches the Tory Burch black and tan combat boots on my feet. I have on a black jumpsuit that cinches in the waist and has skinny leg pants. I look pretty good, if I don't say so myself. My hair is pulled into a semi-messy bun, and my Ray-Ban Aviator rests on my face. In true Label Ladies fashion, my friend Trina decided that just because we were not doing the usual Label Ladies brunch did not mean we could not still dress in labels that match. My girl and her name-brand labels. Trina really can't help herself. She went so far as to say combat boots and all black. She said this make-over was going to be war. She better be glad I love her because I was like, 'Excuse me.'

Anyway, I am back in my SUV and driving to our meet spot. We decided to meet at a boutique first instead of the Galleria. The boutique is called Ebony Elegance. It is a high-end black-owned boutique. It is gorgeous, from the black stained wood and glass front doors, which make you feel like you are entering a palace, to the turquoise-colored chaises with black embroidery to the handmade and intricately designed clothes to the excellent customer service. The ambiance makes you want to go in and spend money. The owner did that!

I pull up to Ebony Elegance just as Erica does, and Trina and Lyric are at Lyric's car talking. We all followed the given clothing instructions and looked like a girl spy group ready to investigate and mess up somebody's man. I get out of the car, chuckling about that fact. As soon as they see my hands hold goodies, here they come.

"Hey, Boo! Oh, you better have brought some food. Got us out here at 9am on a Saturday." Trina starts as I hug her and hand her her favorite chocolate truffle protein smoothie. There are fruits and veggies in it, but it tastes like dessert, which is why we love Jazzy's. You can be as clean and as sweet as you want.

"You know she was over talking about you. This one is not the morning person. And we know this." Lyric says, taking her drink and hugging me.

"Let's be honest. Shoot, are any of us? That's why everyone's drink has a hit of caffeine."

"Absolutely!" We all toast after I give Erica her drink.

I sit the pastries on the hood of Lyric's car, and we finish making the game plan for the day. We are going here, to the Galleria, and then to the nail and beauty shop for our appointments. The girls have already told the nail technicians and the stylist what to do with my nails and hair, and they say I have no choice but to go with it. I just have to trust them.

"Before we go in here, I want to tell y'all how much I love and appreciate you for always being patient with me and having my back. I know I have been weird for a long time, but I am ready to live again, and this is just the beginning of it."

"We love you. We always got you. Just like you always got us, but please don't wild out like this one," Erica says, pointing to Trina.

We all start laughing as Trina starts twerking with her pregnant belly and all. After our laugh and hug, Lyric says, "Alright, Miss Lady, stop procrastinating. We got you. Trust us, Boo." She smiles at me because she knows that is precisely what I am doing at this point. We throw our trash away and walk into Ebony Elegance.

Chapter 16: Liza

We have been shopping all day. My feet are hurting, but I am so excited. I have a whole new wardrobe. I felt like Julia Roberts in Pretty Woman when she was at the boutique, with all the clothes surrounding me. The only thing was I was paying for it. The ladies bought things too. I am pretty sure every store we went into hit their numbers in that segment. We hit up Saks, Tiffany's, Louboutin, Louis Vuitton, Prada, and Sephora. When I tell you, my style has gone from conservative suits and lab coats to sleek and sexy with a hint of flirtation. My girls took my regular earth tones and added in touches of color. I so love it. My Girls did that. I cannot wait to show Olivier. I want to check in on him, but I don't want to interrupt him and his dad, so I hold off.

The ladies and I just finished a light late lunch and are headed to our final feat, the nail and hair salon. I don't know why I agreed to let them choose and not tell me what. However, they have not steered me wrong today, so I will continue to go along with it. I step into this resort-style spa called Venture. It smells of rose oud and vanilla. I am relaxed and feel sexy all at once. The girls hand me an envelope, and Erica starts to talk.

"Boo, we love you, and we have noticed all your changes. We know that it has not been easy to give up control and be honest about the life you really want and who you have always been. We are so proud of you and wanted to treat you to something nice. So, we paid not only for your hair and nails but also for you to get a hot stone massage, facial, and yoni steam. You deserve to feel pampered, so why not finish it off right."

I feel the tears coming down my face and rush into them for a big group hug. With that, we are all taken to our private locker rooms to change and prepare for our services. I am told that my hair and nails will be done after the facial, massage, and yoni steam and to put on the robe for now. So I do and go out into the lightly lit waiting area.

In the waiting area, only Erica is sitting there drinking tea and scrolling through her phone, probably on Pinterest, knowing her.

"Hey Boo, where is everyone else?"

"They were called back already." She scoots over on the love seat she is sitting on so that we can sit together.

"What you looking at?"

"Pinterest for ideas for my Mom's birthday party"

I told you she was on Pinterest. "That's right. This is her 70th birthday, right?"

"Yeah, she is so stoked. She keeps on telling me all this stuff. I haven't seen her this excited in a while."

"Yeah, I know chemo was hard. But she is in remission, so that is to be celebrated too."

"Absolutely." She goes back to scrolling, and I lean back.

"How is the dating scene going?" I ask. Erica has been trying to actively find a man for a couple of years. I know she goes out, but she always seems so needy about it. We tried to tell her to chill out and let the men come, but that is easier said than done.

She looks up into my eyes, and for the first time today, I notice the sadness behind them. She always does a good job making things not seem as bad as they are, like when her mom was going through chemo. We try and let her have that privacy and just be there when she is ready, but I wish she would lean on us more. Then again, I am one to talk. It took me a long minute and a Poweress Mini-Retreat before sharing my truth.

"To be honest, I think I need to redo the celibacy thing."

I take a beat before I say anything because I want to be helpful and not hurtful. I sit up and turn to her. Looking her in the eye, I say, "Erica, you know I love you, and I say this out of love. But your journey to self-discovery did not work that way the last time. What will be different this time?"

"I don't know." She shakes her head, and her shoulders drop in defeat. She puts her phone in her robe pocket.

I scoot closure and I lift her chin. "Boo, all I am saying is if you do it, there needs to be a new intention for it. Last time you said it was to find you, but I really think it was to figure out exactly what kind of man you wanted."

She looks at me, and I can see the tears forming. I bring her in for a tight hug.

"Liza, I just want what all of you have. I know that y'all have all had ups and downs in your relationships, but I want someone who is there to take care of me and love me. A companion and a friend." She leans back and looks at me. "Is that too much to ask for?"

"No. Boo, it is not."

"Then what am I supposed to do?"

"Honestly?"

"Yeah."

"Be true to yourself. Really and truly, learn to be ok in your skin and love yourself. Stop trying to impress these men. Learn to love yourself and know that you have as much to offer as they do. You have to be confident in yourself and your worth. Celibacy is good. You know I believe that. But, if you are going to do this, channel that energy to building your confidence and creating the you that God intended for you to be, not the you who you think a man would want. Come on, Eric. It is time to be Poweress, for real."

"But I try to be me, and they don't seem to like it."

"That means you are looking in the wrong place. Erica, a man that finds a wife, finds a good thing. Stop looking, and learn to be. None of us were looking for our husbands, especially not Trina." We both laugh at that. "But, they all showed up when it was the exact time for us, when we were ready, not just to receive our husband's love but give it in return. When we were ready, not just to let him pay bills but lead us. You get what I am saying?"

"Yeah, when it is my time, it is my time. I need to work on myself in the meantime." She shakes her head.

"No, not just work on you, but love and accept you. Men find confidence sexy. It is not your clothes or your walk or your words. It is the confidence that you know who you are and all others can eat it. Don't work on yourself like something is wrong with you. Accept and love you, and settle for no less than you deserve. That is what I am saying."

She smiles at me. "You said that last part with conviction. It sounded like the Liza I met in graduate school."

"Yeah, she is coming back." We laugh. "I meant what I said, though. You deserve amazing, and he is coming. God is just making y'all ready."

"I agree with you, and I think you are right. I did not really try to accept myself last time but to cover myself up. It is time I finally accept and love myself.........I am sorry. We should not be talking about me. Today was about you."

"Gurl, Bye." I smile at her. "We are besties. I got you, and you got me."

"Absolutely." We both say, and then start scrolling on Pinterest for Erica's mom's party.

A few minutes later, our masseuses come to take us to the back.

Chapter 17: Liza

I love going to Miraculous Bliss, my and my besties' regular yoni steam spot, but this place was on point today. They crystal infused my steam with carnelian, and I feel all kinds of boss lady energy right now. My massage was relaxing, and the facial had my skin glowing. After my steam, now my yoni and my spirit are ready too.

I sit in my pedicure seat, and the technicians give me two color options. I told them whichever one the ladies chose was fine. The nail technician starts on my toes, and the other technician preps my nails for Gel polish. I lean back and just let them work. I think I fall asleep because a little while later, the technician gently shakes my shoulder and tells me it is time for my hair. I smile up at her. As we walk to the washing bowl, I look at my hands. My nails are polished in a beautiful shade of mint green with a design of a little beaker with white and silver glitter inside and sparkles overflowing out of it. As the sparkles come out of the beaker, they turn into stars. The design is on my ring finger, and the other fingers have silver glitter on top of the mint green. My pinky has a double "L" written in black script. My toes are mint green with silver glitter with the small double "L" design on my big toe.

"Do you like it?" The nail tech asks.

"Yes, I love it. Thank you." I laugh.

"Great, the hairstylist will be in in a minute."

The stylist comes and washes my hair, which sends my hair from bone straight to its natural curly pattern. The stylist takes me to her seat but makes me face out so that I cannot look into the mirror. I hear her take out the scissors, and I start to shake my head. I knew they would cut my waist-length hair. They have been trying to get me to change my hair for a minute. I get it. I have had the same hairstyle since college, except for when it is curly.

"Are you okay with this?" The stylist asks.

"Yeah..." I say reluctantly. "Just do it."

She chuckles and gets to work. I see my beautiful tresses falling to the floor. I start to cry not because of the hair that is gone but because of the weight that is leaving me, both physically and spiritually. I hear that soft voice say, "I got you. Honesty gets the truth, and the truth sets you free."

I take the tissue the stylist hands me and take a deep breath. God is right. By being honest with myself, I could tell the truth to those around me, and it has indeed set me free. I hear the stylist mixing. I can only imagine what is next.

After a series of washes and dryer sessions, the stylist puts the finishing touches on my hair, and the make-up artist works a little magic. Then, I hear the stylist call in the ladies. When my girls walk in, their jaws drop.

"Yaasss!!!! Gurl, Yaasss!!" Trina yells and snapping her fingers.

"Boo, you look so bomb!!" Lyric screams.

"Oh, my Gaud, Liiizzzaa!!" Erica exclaims.

With all of their oohs and ahhs, I feel my face heating. I know I am so red by this point. My light skin never hides anything.

"Y'all stop! I will be too red to know how I look," I say.

They laugh at me. Then the stylist whispers. "You ready?"

After a deep breath, I am about to say yes when the girls stop me again.

"Listen, we know you are just going home, but we have a gift for you. We saw you eyeing something at the store, but you wouldn't buy it. And knowing what we had planned here, we all decided to do a thing. So before you look, let's change your clothes to get the full effect. Ok?" Lyric says.

I arch an eyebrow and stand. It is crazy how much your hair actually weighs, but you don't feel it. I feel so light and free with this new hairdo, and I have not even seen it. The ladies present me with a garment bag. I open the bag to find a black sheer corseted tulle cocktail dress with crystals accents in the corset and a slight puff to the skirt from Ebony Elegance. They are right, I was considering buying this but the corset's sheerness gave me pause.

"You guys." I smile.

"Oh, we not done." Trina pulls out a shoebox from Christian Louboutin.

"Trina!"

"Now you know, I think a look is not finished without a pair of red bottoms."

I open the box and find a pair of red sole black wrap sandals. They are gorgeous, I will admit, but they are higher heels than I usually wear.

"How am I to walk in these, Trina?"

"Like the Bad Bitch you are, Liza." She states matter-of-factly. The other ladies laugh.

As I put on the dress, Erica goes to my SUV to get something. She comes back with the three karat pink diamond earrings I splurged on and the matching right-hand ring. I smile at her as she helps me to put them on.

"Liza, you look amazing. I am so happy for you." Erica gives me a hug. The stylist and the technicians come around the divider and oh and ah at my new ensemble. After a moment, I tell them I am ready to see my new self. The stylist leads me to the extravagant floor-to-ceiling mirror in the spa's salon. When I look at myself, I am blown away. I look downright amazing. From the Louboutin's on my feet to the curve of my calves that the heels create, to the gorgeous dress laying on my body that accents my waist, pushes up my breast, and shows the curve of my back enough that you know I definitely have a round backside to the contrast of the black against my ivory skin to the hint of pink in the diamonds to the pink on my lips and rose blush on my cheeks to the smokey eye shadow around my green-hazel eyes to my newly short natural curly mahogany brown hair with honey blonde dipped ends. I look totally different, unique, and utterly me. I step closer to the mirror and take myself all the way in once again. The thought going through my mind is *I am bomb, for real.*

I smile brightly and look at my girls through the mirror with tear latent eyes. They all come and hug me.

"Y'all did this. Real talk. I look all things grown and sexy, Liza."

They all laugh.

"Honey, you need to be going out tonight." The stylist says.

"You are right. I might just pull up on my husband at this event."

All my girls and I say, "Absolutely," and we laugh.

After we checkout and gather everything, we head to our cars and say our goodbyes. I thank them all again and get into my blacked-out black Range Rover Velar HST. I reach in the back, take out my new Alexander McQueen black and silver clutch, and switch out my purse. As I am doing this, I am trying to figure out where I am going. Trina and Lyric had to get back. Trina to get off of her pregnant feet and Lyric to get back to her kids, which is something I do not have to worry about tonight. Erica had to check on her mom. So here I am. As I am thinking, the ladies call me.

"Gurl, can we go, please?" Trina says.

"Sorry, Boo, I was changing purses and figuring out where I am headed. Y'all have me too cute to go home alone. Y'all can leave. I am ok."

"You sure?" Erica says.

"Yeah, go ahead. Thank y'all again."

"Ok," they all say. We say bye again, and then they hang up and pull out of the parking lot. I am about to text Olivier because he should be at the event by now. But before I can, my phone rings again.

"I said I am good," I say, laughing and assuming it is probably Lyric calling me back.

"You sound like you had a great time today." Comes Olivier's smooth baritone through the car speaker, instead. He sounds weary.

"Hey, I was about to text you. Are you okay?"

"No, Belle. I'm not. Can you come to this event tonight? I know..."

I cut him off. "Of course, say less. See you in a few."

"Thanks."

"Love you."

"Love you, too." With that, we hang up, and I pull out of the parking lot. That settles where I am going, and this dress is actually perfect for the formal event that I am now headed to.

Chapter 18: Olivier

The conversation with my Father was beyond difficult. He showed me pictures of him and my birth Mother together at Jazz Fest and Essence Festival in New Orleans. He told me about falling in love with her free spirit and love of people. When he talked about her, there was so much awe and love still laced in his voice. I could understand why my Mother, Lady LeBlanc, told him he could not discuss my birth Mother. He was in love with my birth Mother. The way he described their time together sounded like they were soul mates, two sides of the same coin. Where he was poised and conservative, she was free and uplifting. Where he followed the rules to the utmost, she broke the rules and made her own. She was a singer and songwriter. She taught music at Tulane, in the department right next to his. They met at lunch, and then it became a daily meeting, which turned into happy hours and dinners on the weekends and eventually lovemaking through the nights.

He said he never intended to fall in love with her because he and Lady LeBlanc had an arranged marriage. They were both from prominent families who had run their perspective chapters for generations. To ensure its continuation, their parents arranged their marriage, and my Father and Lady LeBlanc agreed.

Father said when he met my birth Mother, he was not in love with Antonia. He liked her, but that was it. He and Antonia rarely talked about anything that interested him; everything was always about Antonia and what she wanted. This contrasted greatly with the time he spent with my birth Mother. With her, he had such a genuine connection; it was like a breath of fresh air. He said she soothed his heart and nurtured his soul with her love. As much as they tried to break it off after my Father married Lady LeBlanc, he said he could not stay away, especially after finding out she was pregnant. He was like a moth to a flame. The breakup they instilled only lasted seven months, and then he was right back in my birth Mother's company.

He was overjoyed that she was pregnant with me. He wanted to be able to have the family he wanted with my Mother and keep up appearances for the Order with Antonia. Antonia was not on board with this idea, even though she did not love him either. At that, he was ready to leave Antonia and run away with my birth Mother, but his parents threatened to cut him off. He had not made it to tenure professor status yet, and without their funds, he would not be able to support my birth Mother and me the way he wanted to. Therefore, he stayed married to Antonia. After I came, Antonia found out about me, and things got extremely hard for him. He had to take a step back from my birth Mother so that Antonia would not out his affair to the school and the Order and get him removed from both. Dad would go out after the house was sleeping and see my birth Mother. It was hard, he said.

The more he told me, the more I realized that I was so much like my birth Mother. The things that he loved about her were the exact things that got me in trouble as a youth and after college. It was the things he allowed Antonia to scold me about, making me feel out of place and less than. I paced my Father's office as he told me about family members I had never met that had died and passed on. Taking my opportunities for growth and knowledge about myself and my birth Mother with them. At the end of our conversation, he handed me a letter from my birth Mother.

He said she asked him to give it to me when he thought the time was right. He thought today, the time was right.

Once we ended the conversation, I went to one of the guest rooms and dressed. Then we both headed out in silence, going in our separate cars to end up at the same event. We were set to arrive about three hours early to assist with last-minute setups.

The whole drive to the event, I thought about the letter in my pocket and everything that my father had said. I had so many emotions I did not expect to have. I thought the conversation would be challenging because of the topics, but the slew of emotions bombarding me was a shock. Honestly, they were taking me by storm, and the letter in my pocket felt like extra weight. I knew that I needed to read it, but I also knew where I was supposed to be and the things I needed to be able to do tonight.

We had decided to use a ballroom instead of the Club because the Festival of Lights was a charity event, so members and non-members were in attendance. As the venue came into view, I made a choice to give myself a moment for myself, which is something I do not normally do. I usually take my shit and hide it within until the rare moment when I have time to only deal with myself. Today, I am choosing me. I know that the event should be good with my mom and Christy setting up, and I did all the checks yesterday. So my late arrival should not be an issue. I pull into the back of the venue in a covering out of sight and then shoot the President a text.

Hey Union, I need to handle something so I will not make it until right before we are set to start. Is everything good?

Ok. No problem. Ur mom got everything running like a well-oiled machine over here.

I expect nothing less. See u later.

Peace.

I sit in the back parking lot thinking about everything that my dad said and all the information he gave me. He gave me a box of my birth mother's things, which he had hidden in a safe until we eventually had today's conversation. He did hold up his end of the bargain. I will give him that. He answered every question and was genuinely transparent, to the point that I now had all this shit in my head. Now, I am sitting here thinking about the weight in my pocket from this letter from my birth mom. The question is should I open the letter or not? On the one hand, if I go ahead and do it, then maybe I will get the resolve that I am still missing. On the other hand, I already have all of this other shit going through my mind and my heart. About that, I can be honest.

Fuck it. I choose myself today. Not the Order, not my father, me. I am going to read this letter. I undo my seatbelt and pull the letter out of my jacket pocket. I open the envelope, and I pull out the letter. The letter smells of honey and lavender. It is sweet and calming. It feels like home in a way I have never felt before, and instantly I know it is my birth mother's scent. The scent makes me want to cuddle in and allow someone to rub my back and tell me it will be ok. It soothes the deepest corners of my heart and my being. I feel the tears before I even realize I am crying.

I may not remember her, but my body sure does. It is like coming home from being away far too long. I pull the letter to my nose and allow the scent to do what it is doing. After a moment, I open the letter and begin to read.

My sweet Olivier,

If you are reading this, you are probably a grown man with kids, knowing your father. Don't be mad at him. I am sure he handled this the best he could. He is a good man with a big heart. It just takes a moment for him to let someone in and love him. I pray that by the time you are reading this, your father has finally learned to love Antonia and allow her to love him in return. To be honest with you, she is not all bad. I spoke with her about you, about her being your mother when I am gone. I pray she did a good job, that she loved you like her own.

Sweet Olivier, I am so sorry I have not been there to teach you to play the piano, teach you to sing, teach you to shoot for the stars and to be unapologetically you. You have been my music baby from the womb. Whenever I played anything, you danced in my belly. As an infant, you smiled every time I sang to you and even tried to sing back. When you got old enough, I wanted to buy you a guitar so you and I could write music together. You seemed to like the guitar more than the piano when I played.

I got sick a little after you were born and tried to make the best of our time together. There is so much I want to tell you about me, but your father promised to tell you everything we talked about and give you all the items I set aside for you. So what I will say is this, Olivier, be honest with yourself and follow your heart. Holding on to things does not get you better but weighs you down. Know that it is okay to be yourself, unapologetically Olivier Dante LeBlanc. Show the world who you are, even if your family is the one who cannot see it. I pray that one day you find the kind of love that your father and I shared, as unorthodox as it was. You deserve the love of a good woman, for her to respect, love, and support you, to be the helpmate God intended. Don't run from her love, and always let her know you love her and how you feel. Know that you are never alone. God is always with you, and so am I, in those eyes that match mine, in that smile that matches mine, and in that heart that stole mine the moment I laid eyes on you. I am so proud of you. I don't need to see what you have accomplished to know that just you being you is enough for me to say I am proud of you.

I love you, Olivier. Forever and always.

I read the letter three times with more tears streaming down my face each time. I lean my head back. I don't know how, I guess a mother knows, but in that letter, she told me everything I have been trying to believe from the moment I learned of her existence.

I don't know how long I have been sitting in the car crying and thinking. I look at the clock. Shoot, I have been here longer than I thought. I know I need to deal with this shit running through me mentally, physically, and emotionally, but I will have to deal with this later. I need to be inside in ten minutes and be ready to start the auction and the event. I take some deep breaths and center myself. I ask God for help. I push my feelings to the back of my mind and neutralize my face. I make sure that no one can tell I have been in my blacked-out black Audi RS Q8, crying my eyes out. I place the letter back in the envelope and put it in the glove compartment. I look in the mirror one more time, ensuring that all of my shit has been securely tucked away and that my face is neutral. The mirror confirms it, and I am ready to play my part for tonight.

Chapter 19: Olivier

Everything looks immaculate, but I expect nothing less from my mother and sister.

"Hey, stranger. Long time no see. You're late." Christy says as she walks up to me, eyeing my custom three-piece mint green suit and crisp black dress shirt. My tie has a slight pattern embroidered in black satin. There is a matching handkerchief in my breast pocket, and my shoes match the design. I give her a little shove for calling out my lateness. She shoves me back and says,

"Really, Dante, Mint? Like, is it Easter?"

"Funny Big Head, I look good," I say, smoothing out my vest with black buttons.

"I guess. Where is my girl?"

"You know Liza does not like these things. Plus, she was busy today."

"Oh, yeah!! The make-over. Plus, she probably didn't want to come because you look like Easter in October." I give her a little shove again as we laugh.

Mother walks up, bringing both of us to silence. "You look wonderful as always, Dante. Christy, please stop with the antics. You know how I feel about that during Order business."

"Mom, you do realize he is the Vice here. He technically could pull rank on me."

I kiss both of their foreheads before saying, "But you know I won't. Things look beautiful, ladies. Are we ready to start?"

I look around, and the crowd is continuing to grow. I am sure that with the numbers here, we have already met our donation goal, and the night should go smoothly. I look back to see my mother staring at me. Christy is off talking to dad.

"Are you ok, Dante?"

"Yeah, why do you ask?" I don't know why I said that. She may not have given birth to me, but she has known me almost my whole life. She has always been able to read me. She narrows her eyes. Then leans in to whisper, "Have you been crying, Olivier?"

Oh no, her Olivier is always either from anger or concern. The way she is narrowing her eyes at me, it could be from either one of those things.

"It is allergies. You know how Houston is. It has my eyes watery and red. I need to get some eyedrops. Maybe, I will get Liza to pick up some."

"Yes, the pollen here is horrible. I do miss New Orleans in that regard. Where is Liza?"

"Taking care of some things. Let me go get us started, and I will be back." I say as the President waves me over.

After introducing the silent auction and officially opening the event, the bar is opened, and the dancing and networking begin. I make my rounds. But it seems like the more hands I shake, the more unnerved I become. When I get back to my mother, I feel sweaty and uneasy. My father walks up and gives me a knowing look, and I see my mother assessing our nonverbal exchange.

"Would one of you like to talk about whatever is going on here?" She says with that Lady LeBlanc no-nonsense tone.

My father looks at her, and I can see the love and compassion that he has for her now that he did not have at the time of my birth. Part of what he told me was that he eventually did learn to accept Antonia for who she is and love her. By the time he did that, Christy was born. I watch him ease her thoughts about there being no issues between us and lead her off to meet some of the members from the Dallas chapter. I take a breath, walk to the side, and lean on the wall. Honestly, I do realize that I am barely holding it together.

I see Christy headed toward me when I look up, "Hey, aren't you supposed to mingle and make people feel welcomed?"

"I did that already. I will make rounds again in a second."

"I can't believe this is you now."

"I know, me either, but such is life."

"I have missed you guys." She says, looking up at me. I smile.

"We have missed you too. But that is what happens when you get married and move to Chicago."

"True......" We stand in silence for a while. The longer she stands there with me, the more unsettled I become. I cannot help but think about the fact that she has no idea how unideal our family really is. She has never known my struggle, nor does she know that my mother is not her mother. This is making my head spend with other thoughts about the letter. Why did I think I could do this today? I know why because I am usually really good at acting fine when I am not. Well, I guess not this time. I take a deep breath and see her side-eye me. I am sure that I look close to being a neutral wall on the outside like always, but I am a hair away from that no longer being the case.

"Dante, do you think we can all go out to dinner before I leave? You know the whole family?"

Before I can stop my thoughts, I think, *the whole family? Minus the other piece of my family.* Wow, that is a new reaction. I need to get some air.

So I say, "Yeah, sounds great. Let me know when, and I and the fam will be there. I will be right back."

She looks at me sideways a little bit. Yeah, I am sure my façade is falling now. I get outside and go to the back of the building but keep an eye on the front. I am supposed to be in my Vice-President position right now. I take some deep, clearing breaths and ask God to help me. Then I hear that soft voice say, "Call your wife."

Right. I pick up the phone and call Liza. Thankfully she agrees to come to meet me without asking lots of questions.

I don't think I could have answered her questions without falling apart. My façade would be obliterated talking to her, but at the same time, right now, I need her.

Chapter 20: Olivier

I see Liza parking, and I shoot her a text letting her know where I am standing outside. As I am propped up against the corner of the building, ready to watch her get out of the car, someone taps my shoulder, so I turn around. It is one of the chapter officers asking me to sign some papers for tonight and agree to the amended budget. Even though I am Vice, I basically do all the presidential duties because the chapter is still new.

I hear heels clicking on the pavement behind me and turn around, and I am speechless. The woman walking toward me is a vixen. From the 6-inch stilettos on her feet to the sheer corset at her waist to the gorgeous cleavage asking for me to take a sample to the sultry look in her eyes to the blonde tips of her short hair, this woman is all things indescribably, intoxicatingly erotic and delectable. So much so that I am speechless. She stands before me with a slight smirk. She lets me take her in slowly. Allowing me to walk around her and indulge my eyes in all that she is and all that she is offering. I can see her skin reddening the more I peruse her body with my eyes. I step into her space on my second trip around, allowing my suited chest to touch her bareback. Then I lean in, lightly lick her ear, and blow ever so softly. She shivers slightly, enough that only I can see.

Then I whisper, "Liza.....Daammn!" I kiss her shoulder and then continue. "You look amazingly gorgeous. I don't know if I want to show you off, eat you right here, or take you home. Belle, this is absolutely everything."

She leans her head back slightly so that my mouth touches her ear, "So, you like it?"

I take her hand and press it into my hardened erection. She turns fire engine red, the exact reaction I want. "Like does not even begin to describe how I feel."

She turns around to look me in the eye, but then she sees the reason I called. It is the reason I have been standing behind her. As much as I am intoxicated by my wife right now, I knew the moment she looked into my face, she would know something was wrong. These women in my life notice everything. The difference is that Liza is my woman, and I know that my feelings and my heart are safe with her. So when she asks me things like what I know is coming, everything in me wants to tell her and let her do just as my birth mother said to let her love and support me.

"Olivier, what's wrong?"

"It was a lot, Belle." She has stepped into my space and is holding my hand between us.

"The conversation?"

"Yeah...... I thought I would be able to shake it until this was over, but....." I trail off and let my head fall as I shake out a no.

She gently raises my chin. She smiles at me softly. "What do you need? We can blow this joint, and you can blame me if you want?" She chuckles.

"I would love to, but you know I can't." I sober, trying to re-neutralize my face.

"Ok, then, we go back in there, and you dance with me like no one else in that room even exists. Can you do that?"

"Always." I can easily get lost in her. It has happened many times before.

"Good," With that, she runs her hand from my hand to my biceps and pulls me into her, and we start to walk. She stops me before we reach the front. She says, "Olivier, you are amazing. Just you being you is enough. Your Mother would be proud."

I smile into my wife's beautiful face and know that everything will be okay. As long we continue to love each other, be honest with ourselves, and be truthful with each other, we will be able to make it through whatever storms come.

I kiss her softly and say, "Thank you, Belle. I love you, forever and always."

"I like that. I love you too, forever and always."

We share one more kiss and then go into the event and dance the night away, like no one else in the room exists but her and me.

The End.

Epilogue: Liza

6 Months Later

Things have been really great. Olivier decided that he would start going to individual counseling. He realized that just having the information about his birth mother was not enough for him to have the resolve that he needed and wanted fully. Even though he didn't want to hold things against his parents, he was. He realized he resented them to some degree for keeping this from him. If he had not told me how he felt, I would not know by the way he acts with them because he is still loving and kind. But that is Olivier, well it was Olivier. Therapy has been genuinely helping him. He decided to do his therapy with a male therapist instead of our couples counselor, Dr. Judy. He said there were some things he needed to say he didn't feel comfortable speaking to her about. She understood and gave him a referral.

We still go to couples counseling, but now we go once a quarter, which is a true accomplishment from our weekly therapy sessions. Our marriage has been beautiful, from communication to compromises to making love. I could not ask for more. My babies are getting bigger, healthier, and happier than ever before, and I am thankful for that.

These are all of my reflective thoughts as I drive to Label Ladies. I have on a black double-breasted Saint Laurent coat dress with a pair of custom black and rhinestone sheer six-inch pumps and my black Saint Laurent envelope clutch. Hey, it is Label Ladies. I have to be cute. Honestly, I always feel sexy and free, naked or clothed, since my make-over.

At Label Ladies, we have started doing other things plus brunch. We needed more time together than we had been giving ourselves. Once a quarter was no longer enough, from Trina having baby Isaiah, to me and Lyric's kids growing up, to Erica deciding what needed to happen to change her life. We just needed more time together.

I pull up to the upscale lounge that Trina picked, of course. Getting married did not change Trina, just who she is wild with. Anyway, it is a lovely space. There is a floor-to-ceiling glass window on one side of the lounge, and you can see the purple and blue lights flickering inside. Trina said at night, they raise the shade of the floor-to-ceiling window so that you can see the city no matter where in the lounge you are. It is a three-story lounge with different liquor mixtures and music on each floor. I walk in, and there are my girls in their Saint Laurent and looking oh so beautiful.

"Gurl, you better give me thighs!!" Trina yells as she comes to hug me in her bandage dress with Saint Laurent heels.

"Hey, Boo!!" Erica and Lyric chime in. They look gorgeous in their pants and crossbodies from Saint Laurent. It always amazes me when we do Label Ladies that as much as we hang out, we never actually have on the same items from the designers we wear.

After our hugs and hellos, Trina takes us to the third floor, which is having a neo-soul night. So, we can just groove and chill. The third floor's lights are dim, and there is hookah in one corner and the sweet smell of vanilla oud in the air. There are deeply colored love seats, ottomans, and chaises set up in front of crystal and wood coffee tables. There is a stage set up in the front, and the bar is off to the side. The vibe is chill and relaxing. Honestly, it kind of reminds me of the New Orleans Club of the Order on the night I met Olivier.

After we order drinks, we head to a section in the corner lit by candlelight and has plush dark green love seats. Once our drinks arrive, we do our catch-up.

Trina and Jackson are still madly in love. She is thinking about doing a couples trip to Jamacia, but she will let us know. Our little god-baby, Isaiah, is doing so well too. He looks just like Jackson.

"How is business?" Lyric asks

"Amazing!! You know Ms. Kathy and I bumped heads at first, but I think we have finally found our lanes. As long as she is over there, we are good." We all laugh. Next up is Lyric.

"Everything is good on this front. No real news. Sorry ladies. Eze is still my amazing and annoying, at times, husband and the kids are growing more and more. The business is sick in the best of ways. I couldn't ask for more. Erica?"

"Well, you know I am working on myself. Trying that whole accept and love me thing. I have not sworn off men, just not pursing anymore."

"Praise God," Trina says.

"Shut up," I say, elbowing her. "Keep going, Erica. You know she is missing some pieces."

Lyric laughs. Trina kicks her.

"Like I was saying, children...." We all laugh. "Sorry, Ms. Erica." Trina and Lyric say.

"Y'all are a mess....... So, I was thinking the Poweress Committee sent an email for a Friends-Only Cruise Adventure. I do not know what the specific theme is. They are being oddly vague about this one, but I feel like I need to be there for some reason. Do y'all want to go? It is in 3 months, and I feel like I need this in a way that I didn't need the others. I feel a sense of urgency. You know?"

Lyric, Trina, and I look at each other with a knowing smirk because that is the exact feeling we all had when we went to our retreats and God changed our lives. So, what else can we say to our girl about going other than, "Absolutely."

We all clap hands and agree to book the cruise when we make it home. We enjoy the rest of our night out, drinking, dancing, and having a great time with each other.

As I drive home, tired but rejuvenated, I can say it was good to be honest with myself. Being honest has truly changed my life in the most marvelous of ways. As I am letting this revelation marinate within me, my phone rings. It is Olivier. He should be sleeping.

"Hey," is all he says in that beautiful baritone when I accept the call.

"Hey, yourself. Everything alright?"

"Yeah, I just finished doing something I have not done in a while."

"Which was?"

"I wrote a song."

"Really!! That's great!" I say as I turn down our street.

"The song is for you," he drops his baritone voice an octave with that statement. I lick my lips. He knows I love it when his voice gets that deep.

"Belle, are you almost here?"

"Yes."

"Good because I am waiting to sing it to you. Do you want to hear it?" He is seducing me, and he knows it is working. I can tell by the smile in his voice. I open the garage, and there he is, standing in nothing but a towel with his locs cascading down his shoulders. He has a phone in one hand and the guitar he customized and dedicated to his mother in the other hand.

"Belle, you didn't answer me. Do you want to hear it?" He is smiling at me with those perfectly white teeth of his.

"Yes." I practically moan into the phone as I cut off the car and close the garage.

"Good, meet me in the bedroom." With that, he smirks at me and drops his towel. He waits until my eyes reach his deliciously hardened erection, and I moan into my phone. I see him smile wider at my reaction. He then ends the call and walks away, holding nothing but his guitar.

Oh yea, honesty has been good to me!

Note from the Author

Thank you for taking this journey with me to share in the love and growth of Liza and Olivier, aka Dante. I will be honest with you. This book was a little hard for me. However, I wanted to make that we get an accurate picture of love within marriage when the struggle is not about money, drugs, or cheating. As you saw, marriage has its own set of issues, and it takes time, effort, and love to keep it going, and, of course, God. I hope you fell in love with Liza and Olivier's love, passion, and intensity. I also hope that you got the revelation as I did; honesty with yourself is one of the most incredible things you can give to yourself. As you are honest with yourself, you can be truthful with others, and that truth genuinely sets you free. As always, thank you for reading and taking this journey of honesty with me.

Please lookout for the next and last book in this series, Power of Acceptance, Erica's story.

Peace and Love, Minniel

P.S. If you are interested in experiencing the beauty and clarity of Medivotion or the healing and revelation of Reiki, or if you need a Life Coach to help walk out the words God has already planted within you, please go to my website, www.peacebeloved.co and book a session in-person or virtual. We also have party sessions, so you and your girls or you and your partner can have a spiritual moment together. I look forward to taking the journey of Poweress with you.
Peace, Beloved.